The gift of a magical self-help book changes the lives of each woman who receives it. These powerful stories show that falling in love is not a sign of weakness, but the greatest gift of all. Pick your journey and open your heart to the incredible power hidden deep inside each of us.

Her heart was scared, and Catarina felt a little charred from all the drugs, pain, and shit life had thrown at her. But one book, three little orphans, and the hottest man Catarina had seen in a long time changed her belief in happy ever after.

Arad Carf had a life, but when his wife had been murdered long ago, his heart had stopped beating. Even with family, grandchildren all around him, nothing had gotten his old heart pounding again until he saw her, Catarina.

Was she the warrior woman Arad Carf would need at his side? Could she measure up, not to mention, raise his three grandchildren along with her two if they found them?

Catarina
Finding the Warrior's Heart: 2

By

Trinity Blacio

Chapter One

Catarina Wahlberg stared out at the Trinity Bay, wrapping her coat tighter around her. It was still early, and the three children she had agreed to take in were still asleep. She had stayed up half the night reading the book that had been sent to her. From whom she had no idea, but now, she wouldn't give the book back even if it wasn't meant for her, but the book did have her name in it.

She snorted and glanced back at the house. Even though Catarina had snuck out, she had no doubt that the children had heard her leave to come out here for her morning cleansing. The fresh air, no matter how cold, always showed her that she was still alive, even after all that she had gone through.

Being one of the only humans in a city of wolves and bears, Catarina had settled there three years ago, finally feeling safe. At thirty-three, Catarina had lost her two babies, six years ago when the courts had agreed with their father. That she, their mother, had no say in the raising of her daughters after her ex had found out about her prison time.

Of course, living in a town where Andrew knew everyone and was a good old boy also did not help. A tear rolled down her cheek, and she went to wipe it away when Catarina heard the boy, Marcus, behind her as he cleared his throat.

"I'm fine, Marcus, just remembering," she said and looked over her shoulder at the handsome little man. He would be a powerful man when he grew up, she could already tell by the way he held himself and protected his sisters, and even her now.

The three didn't say much, giving the town only their first names when they had been found scrounging up food. At first, the mayor or beta wolf had thought to break up the three, but Catarina, hearing the news, asked if she could have them stay with her until their family could be found.

Marcus stepped up next to her and took her hand, holding it. "You miss your two little girls?" he asked.

"Every single day. Most humans forgive past mistakes, but not always," Catarina said, squeezing his hand.

"That's why you told that man about your past, so they wouldn't hold it against you?" he asked, smarter than she had realized.

"Yes, something like that. I didn't want to see the three of you separated. No one should be separated from their family. Come, it's getting cold, and I'm sure you and your sisters are hungry as the bears next door."

Marcus snorted. "Never that hungry. I've never seen someone eat so much." He laughed.

"You and me both, little man, you and me both," Catarina said when she noticed the mail lady walking toward them.

"I thought I would bring the mail by and see how your three houseguests are doing," Frita said, smiling down at Marcus. "You three settling in?" she asked Marcus.

Marcus frowned. "We are fine. Miss Cat is great, and she can cook."

Frita laughed. "Well, then I'm glad my husband agreed for you to come here. We're still hoping to find your family one day."

Marcus snarled and shook his head. "Catarina will be our family. Don't want anyone else."

"Easy there, Marcus." Catarina knelt down next to Marcus. "I'm not going anywhere, but Marcus, remember what I told you, not all is what is it seems. Okay?" she asked, and he nodded.

"But I still don't want to leave. Our Momma is dead," he said, giving them something for the first time in two months to go on. "He killed her, our father. We have no one but you." Marcus wrapped his arms around her neck, giving her a hug.

"I'm so sorry, little man, so sorry." Catarina's heart broke, and when she looked up, she could tell that Frita was feeling the same thing.

"I'll let Ronnie know, and Marcus, do not worry, we are not going to separate you. Everyone in town can see how you three are faring." With that, Frita left them alone.

"Come, sausage, pancakes, eggs coming up," Catarina said, hearing Marcus's stomach growl. When she looked up, Catarina smiled, seeing the two little girls, Romy and Little Tee, grinning at her through the door.

"Would you three like to go for a run later? I hear the other children will be going out to the park. I think all of us need to get some exercise.

These rolls aren't going to go away if I sit inside," she mumbled, even though Catarina knew it didn't matter anyway. No man would look at her once they learned what mistakes she had made. Hell, she didn't even know if it was worth risking her heart.

She placed her mail on the counter, wishing for more pictures of her little girls, but so far, her friend hadn't sent her any in over two years.

Catarina glanced at the book on the kitchen table. "Maybe you'll help," she whispered, hoping something would bring back the strong woman she used to be. Hopefully, Delia Winters, Vampire, Psychic warrior would be able to help her.

One dozen eggs, two pounds of bacon, twenty sausage links and over four dozen blueberry pancakes, Catarina was ready for a nap. But all three kids were finally full and smiling. "Okay, Marcus, you help Little Tee get ready for our outing while I get these dishes cleaned up. Romy, do you want to help?" she asked and got a big smile from the older girl.

"I could have helped with the dishes," Marcus said, frowning.

"That you could have, but if I'm not mistaken, Little Tee would like some brotherly attention." Catarina nodded to the little girl who had not spoken yet to anyone. She stood by her chair waiting.

Marcus turned and smiled. "Come on, Little Tee, let's get you dressed."

Catarina laughed, seeing the bubbles all over Little Tee's nose. Marcus had gotten his sister dressed in record time, so all of them had helped washing the dishes. "Okay, dishes are done, and I'm afraid we all need a change of clothes again." She looked down at herself and laughed. She, too, was covered in bubbles and water.

She glanced at the clock on the wall. "We have ten minutes to change clothes. Put the wet ones over the chairs in your rooms. We'll meet back here. Little Tee, you want me to help you?" she asked, but Little Tee shook her head and placed her hand into Marcus's.

"Okay, one step at a time, ten minutes," she said and moved to go to her room. Catarina would read chapter three as she let the kids run and play. She stepped into her bedroom, her gaze going right to the pictures of her babies.

The lump once more appeared in her throat and tears came to her eyes, she missed her babies so much. "No time," she whispered and went to open her dresser when a tiny hand tugged on her shirt.

She looked down to see Tee standing there with her arms up. Catarina knelt down and lifted Tee into her arms. "You knew I was sad, didn't you?" she said, burying her face in the child's neck.

"We can feel it, sense it, I think is the right word," Marcus said as he and Romy came into her room. Can we see the pictures of your little girls?"

"Sure, climb up on the bed, and I'll show you some," Catarina said and placed Little Tee on the bed before turning to grab the photo album she had started of her babies.

Tears running down her face, she smiled at Little Tee and then looked up at Marcus. "Always remember, Marcus, that no matter what one person does, it does not mean that others will do the same thing. We have to learn to trust. If we don't, we will live a very lonely life."

"You would forgive the man that took your babies?" Marcus asked.

"No, but I know other people like him are not to blame for what he did." She sighed. "You see, Marcus, my father was also a mean man, used to beat me whenever he could. I remember going to school with broken ribs but couldn't do anything because my father was an important man for the government."

"Is he still alive? Your father?" Marcus asked.

She frowned. "I have no idea and don't want to know. But if I had any other family who I would have known about back then, I would have gone to them, at least I hope I would have. What I'm trying to tell the three of you is that if your family comes looking for you, as I would if you were my family, you're going to have to go with them."

Marcus jumped off the bed and picked up Little Tee. "No, we stay here and be your children. We have already decided. We'll let you change."

She watched as all three of them left, closing her door. "Wow. Okay, that didn't go over well." Catarina smiled. She loved all three of them already and knew it was going to be hard if they did have family out there.

"No sense in thinking about it now," she mumbled, jumping up and getting dressed, putting her photo album back under her bed for another day.

* * *

Arad Carf turned off his bike, staring down at the little city where his grandbabies were supposed to be. His heart was heavy from finding their mother dead over a hundred miles away. Going to the next city, he had learned about the three children being found and that they were here, safe.

He had camped out two nights, watching and scoping out the city. Now, it was time to go find his grandbabies. Oh, he had caught their scent a number of times, but he would proceed with caution.

"What did you see, little ones? I'm so, so sorry. I promise I'll make it up to you." He started the bike and moved down into the city. It was a nice little city, and from what Arad had found out, a mixture of shifters lived there.

He parked his bike at the sheriff's office and smiled, watching a group of children running on the hill above the city.

"Aww, to be young again. Can I help you, Alpha?" the sheriff said, coming out of the building, holding out his hand. "My name is Ronnie Turns." The wolf sniffed and sighed. "You're here for the three little ones, aren't you?"

Arad nodded. "They are my grandbabies. I found their mother about a hundred miles away from here. I'm afraid my son was one of the ones infected by the humans," he snarled.

"We heard about what happened. Many have lost their lives, but I was also told that the drug only enhanced what was there," Ronnie said, staring at Arad, and he had to smile.

"No, Sheriff, I am not my son. He is dead, killed him myself a few months ago. Been searching for the little ones ever since. Are they hurt?"

"Not physically, but emotionally, yes. I'm not going to mince words here. They are just starting to come out of their shells. Catarina has performed a miracle with the children. Little Tee still won't speak, and Marcus is protective of all of them, including Catarina. He'll be a fine alpha one day. "Come, with me." The sheriff moved down the street toward the hill where the children were playing.

"When we found the children, we had no one that could take all the children in. But Catarina insisted that they stay together, that they needed each other, and she was right. I normally don't place any children with humans, but with her, well, she's special."

Arad stopped and growled. "You placed my grandbabies with a human?"

Ronnie stopped and turned to face Arad. "Yes, Catarina Wahlberg is part of this town, and everyone here would protect her with their lives. In a way, your grandbabies are also healing her heart, too. I would caution how you act around her because if Marcus sees one ounce of threat against her, you'll lose him."

Arad said nothing as Ronnie turned and moved up the hill. As soon as they reached the large open area, a woman came over and wrapped her arms around the sheriff. "Frita, I'd like you to meet..."

"Arad Carf, it's an honor. I remember seeing you one time when my father drove up for one of the meetings. What brings you here?" She looked from him to his grandbabies sitting next to a woman who laughed, ruffling Marcus's hair.

Catarina looked up, and his gaze met hers. Inside, his sleeping wolf rose, shocking the hell out of him. "Please, introduce us."

Ronnie had been right. As soon as they got close, seeing Catarina rise, Marcus stepped in front of her and growled at Arad.

"Don't; we are not leaving. Go home."

"Marcus, remember what I said earlier. You have to hear him out if he is family," the woman said, stepping up, but again, Marcus stepped in front of her.

"Don't get close. He could be like my father. We won't lose you," his grandson said.

Arad stood there staring at the boy. "Right now, I'm not going to take you anywhere. But I will tell you this, son, your father is dead. I found your mother, and she is being taken home to be buried."

Behind Marcus, Little Tee whimpered, and at once, Catarina turned and scooped her up. "Shhh, Little Tee, no one is going to hurt you. I tell you what. Since you three are finished playing, why don't we go to the diner and we can have lunch with your grandfather? You three all love Rose's hamburgers, and you are going to need the food, but we better hurry because I heard the bears were going, too." Catarina glanced over her shoulder at a family.

The lady laughed. "That's right; we might eat all the hamburgers before you even order," the mother teased.

Marcus stared at Arad then at Catarina. "Are you sure you want to do this?"

"Marcus, we'll be in public and surrounded by our friends. Plus, has your grandfather made any threating moves?" she asked.

"No, but we're still not leaving. You need us. We have no mother or father, and you lost your children. We are our family now," Marcus told her, and tears filled the beautiful woman's eyes.

"Marcus," she whispered.

Chapter Two

Catarina was a damn mess. The man across the table from her was the hottest thing she had seen since, well, ever. His green eyes were the most intense, and when he turned them on her, Catarina swore she would melt. But then, there was the fact he was here to take the children she had grown to love. How she was going to get over this one was going to be the question, but then, she remembered the words of Delia.

Lost souls, ancient warriors have the biggest hearts. It takes a great warrior like you to bring the love back into one so broken. You have to decide if you risk it or not.

She shook her head. "Impossible," Catarina mumbled.

"What's impossible?" Arad asked her as once again his attention turned on her.

"Just something I read earlier. So, where is the rest of your family? What happened? I heard bits and pieces, tried to help best I could, too, but I didn't know much," Catarina said, sticking a fry in her mouth. "Eat, Marcus, and quit glaring at your grandfather; it's rude. As you can see, we are surrounded by others, and he hasn't threatened us at all."

"Either did my father until..." Marcus countered as he looked down at his food, picking up a fry and eating it.

Catarina leaned over and placed her hand on Marcus's but looking at the girls also. "Remember our talk. You see how sad I get when I look at pictures or remember my babies?" Both girls nodded and Marcus covered her hand.

"What if I gave up? Where would you three have gone? We all have to take a chance, Marcus." She snorted. "You know the book I got the other day?" Catarina lifted it up, seeing the children nod but wasn't expecting the man across from them to growl.

At once, Marcus was on top of the table in front of her, both girls were climbing over to her, pulling her out of her seat.

"Hurry, we get away now," Romy said, crying and begging her to move.

"Marcus, get down!" Ronnie said, coming over and pulling him off the table. "What is going on?"

"My fault, you were right. I'm afraid my emotions got a hold of me." Arad slid out of his chair and knelt down in front of Marcus, who was snarling. "I wasn't growling to hurt Catarina." He looked back at the book on the table. "Do you mind?" he asked Catarina, nodding to the book.

"No," she said, watching as he picked up her book. "My grandson, your oldest brother Wolf, his mate has one of these books, too. It has some meaning that you wouldn't understand 'til you get older."

"Wolf has a mate?" Marcus asked.

"Yes, and she is something. I think you three will love her. She's also part fae, a princess," Arad said, standing. "I'm sorry I've caused so much ruckus." He turned and handed the book to her.

The sheriff snorted. "So, the rumors are true about the psychic? Interesting. I'll have to tell my wife now." He glanced down at Marcus. "You going to be okay?" he asked Marcus, who nodded but moved in front of Catarina and his sisters.

"I'm trusting you to give your grandfather a chance here, Marcus. We'll speak soon," Ronnie said and moved toward the back of the dinner.

"May I ask why you growled at my having this book? Come on, Marcus, Romy, Little Tee, let's go for a walk and let these people have lunch in peace. Rose, I'm so sorry about the mess." She went to the register. "Please, put the dishes on my bill."

"Oh no, you don't. This is on us, sweetie. You work too hard for what you have. Now, go on, all of you. Wait..." The older lady went into the kitchen and brought out a big basket. "This is for dinner. I know for a fact you love my casseroles. This is a new one I am trying out, so make sure to let me know what you and the little ones think. I've also thrown in a berry pie I made."

"But..." Catarina sighed, seeing Rose's look. "I swear you have that look down pat, thank you, Rose." She leaned over and placed a kiss on Rose's cheek, going to grab the basket, but Arad grabbed it for her.

"I've got it. You have your hands full," he said, his gaze looking at Little Tee and Romy at her side holding onto her tight.

"Thank you. Come, girls, let's walk home. How

about a picnic tonight outside if it stays nice out? Of course, you'll eat supper with us." She looked over at Arad.

"Maybe I should give you a break with the children. I think they have a lot to deal with right now." He held open the door for them.

"Nonsense, you are family, and they need to get used to you. What a better place than where they consider safe," she said, knowing Marcus was staring at him, watching Arad's every move.

"Can I ask what you meant about trying to help when we were attacked?" Arad asked her, and she sighed.

"I'm afraid my past is not so hot. My father is one of those scientists who most likely helped develop whatever it was. He's a nasty man and has a mean left hook, too. Learned that at an early age. Even my mother felt it a few times. I'm not the brain he is, so I was a very big disappointment. I told Ronnie the last place I had seen my father, but of course, the house was vacant. I have no idea where my parents are now and have no desire to see them again. Now, I told you something about me, tell me about the book and why you don't like it?" she asked.

* * *

Arad walked next to his grandbabies, trying to get his wolf under control. When Catarina had mentioned about being beaten by her father, he had almost shifted right there and then.

"Excuse me," Arad got out as he pulled out his

phone that was going off, knowing it was Wolf.

"Wolf," he said, earning looks from all three grandbabies. "I have found your siblings, and they are healthy."

"Marcus, Wolf would like to speak with you," Arad said, holding out the phone to his grandson.

"Can I say hi?" Romy asked, stepping forward.

"Of course, he's missed all three of you. Byron has been going crazy with worry. He misses your nightly chats," Arad said, and his heart broke as tears filled Romy's eyes as she took the phone.

"Wolf," she whispered.

Arad looked up at Catarina. Her blond hair blew around her face as tears rolled down her cheeks as her gaze met his. "It's the first time she's actually reached out. What do you say, Little Tee, you want to say hi to your brother?"

Little Tee buried her face into Catarina's neck, shaking. "It's okay, Little Tee, when you are ready. No one is going to make you do anything, baby," Catarina comforted as Marcus took the phone from Romy.

"He's not sick like daddy was," Romy informed to Catarina. "He wants us to come to his home, but I don't want to. It's scary there."

Arad frowned. "Why would my home be scary? Wolf now lives at my cabin, Romy. It's surrounded by woods, the mountains, and all sort of animals. I really think you will like it."

"This is my home, with Catarina." Romy wrapped her arms around Catarina's waist. "I told Wolf I have a new mommy now."

Marcus came up to Arad and handed him the

phone. "Wolf wants to speak with you."

Arad took the phone and started to walk. "Yes?" he said, knowing exactly what his grandson was going to say.

"*What's going on with my brother and sisters? Who is this Catarina?*" Wolf growled.

"It's the woman they have been living with. They have bonded with her, Wolf. I can't rip them from her, especially considering the trauma they have been through. But that isn't the only thing; I'll explain later."

"*Why was Marcus asking about a book?*" Wolf asked, and he moaned. "*Let me guess, this woman has the same book Tobie has.*" Wolf laughed.

"Shut up, Wolf," Arad snapped and hung up the phone. "Pain in the ass, no respect for elders," he mumbled.

"This way and having problems?" Catarina asked, turning down a side street.

"No, seems both children have told their brother they were staying here," he said.

"I'm sure, in time, when the children get used to their grandfather, they'll be okay," she said. "We're here. Marcus, go feed Hank, please. Romy, let's get some lemonade made; we can sit outside. Little Tee, why don't you go get your tablet, that always soothes you when you read. I'll even get you another story." Catarina placed the child down and watched Tee run into the house if you could call it that.

He was pretty sure the screen door was ready to fall off, the roof looked new, but the siding was falling off in places.

"It might not look the greatest, but it keeps me warm on the coldest nights, and there are the most spectacular views. Plus, it was all I could afford, but it's all mine," Catarina said, going inside, but he had seen the hurt in her eyes, which had his heart breaking.

"Catarina, I meant nothing. Would you like to know what this book is about?" Arad said, coming inside and picking up the book, moving to the kitchen table. "Please, sit, let me explain a few things?" He pulled out a chair and waited.

She stared at him for a minute before nodding and sitting in the chair. "The author of the book, you know, is one of the few psychics in our world. She is helping a few of our men find the woman that is their other half while helping the woman in question at the same time."

Catarina frowned. "And you think that I'm yours? Don't you already have a wife?"

Arad put the book on the table, his heart hurting thinking of his wife. "My wife was killed over ten years ago. It's been rough. Usually, when a mate passes, we just wait for our time together again." He moved to the window above the sink, staring out.

"My wife, Starla, wasn't my mate, but nothing mattered. We loved each other and always believed that our true mates were already walking on the next path." Arad looked over his shoulder.

"I'm so sorry. I know what it's like to lose someone you love," she whispered as Marcus came in.

"What's wrong?" he asked, glaring at Arad.

"Marcus, we are just talking. You need to get

over this now. I will only put up with so much disrespect. I know what you saw and had to deal with was traumatic, but right now, we are all suffering. All of us need to band together if we are going to get through this." Arad held his grandson's gaze for a few seconds until the boy looked down at the ground.

"We're not leaving Catarina. We can't leave her," Marcus said.

"You are right, we can't leave her. I have not said anything about taking you away from her. But we will all need to go back to pay your respects to your momma. Wolf and your other siblings will wait for us. I have a feeling you will like the place where we chose her resting place."

"Not near him," Marcus snarled. "He does not deserve to be next to her."

Arad turned his full attention to Marcus. "Your father did love her, or you wouldn't be standing here. He was sick, Marcus." Arad touched the side of his head. "In here."

"Was it because of what my father and the others did?" Catarina asked.

"Only a fraction actually. It turns out, the original formula was from the fae world. This goes nowhere, Marcus, understand? I'm trusting you here with this knowledge," Arad said, and Marcus nodded right away, stepping closer to him.

"Can they heal those that were infected?" he asked.

"The drug only enhances what was already buried deep in a person's soul. I saw little things about your father when he was growing up but believed he would grow out of it. I was wrong, and then, when he was hit with this drug, there was nothing anyone could have done."

"What about the drug? Is it still around? Do you and they have to worry about getting hit with it?" she asked.

Arad moved back to the table and sat next to Catarina, placing his hand over hers. "The king has removed all traces of the drug from this world, but scientists like your father have the formula and are trying to duplicate it from what we have learned. It would seem a group of individuals that were with the government have branched off and are now trying to destroy what they can of us."

Catarina got up, growling. "God, I hate that man. I wish I could have killed him when I had a chance. Excuse me while I change." She rushed out of the room, and he could see the tears rolling down her cheeks.

"What did you mean we're not leaving Catarina?" Marcus asked, sitting in her seat as the two other little ones came over next to him.

Arad smiled at the three little ones. "Maybe it's Fate's way that the three of you have bonded with this woman because I believe your Catarina is my mate." He stood, moving toward where she had left. Hearing her crying was driving him crazy.

"Don't hurt her?" Marcus said.

"I'm not, my son, believe me, Catarina will be treasured." He left, going to search for his woman, needing to comfort her.

Chapter Three

Catarina stared out at the ocean. After leaving him in the kitchen, she had run out the front door, needing the fresh air. Never had she felt so sick. These people around her had saved her, taken her into their community, and treated her with respect, but yet, her father and men like him wanted to hunt and make sure they were killed.

No, they weren't men, her father and the others were sick excuses of blobs as Romy would say. She smiled, so going to miss the three little ones. They had become part of her heart, and right now, the thought of them leaving was ripping her apart.

"You shouldn't be out here by yourself," Arad said, putting a sweater over her shoulders. "What a view." He wrapped his arms around her and pulled her back into his body.

"Arad?" she looked up at him.

"You're my woman, Catarina, and when you are hurting, I hurt."

"Then, the fates must really hate you because I'm nothing, Arad. I'm just a woman trying to survive day to day and hope I don't slip back into my black days," she said, not having the strength to move out of his arms, wanting to feel safe at least for that minute.

"My grandchildren would not have bound themselves to you, Catarina, if you had a black soul. Now, tell me what are your black days?"

She sighed, he had a right to know if he was really considering this thing, feelings that coursed through her every time he touched or looked at her. "The beatings got worse, and if I went to the doctor or asked for help, it would be worse. Too soon, drugs seemed to be my only way out. My black days, where I don't remember anything, just numb and high." She held out her arms, looking down at the scars from the needles. "See the scars that I inflicted on myself." She turned, moving out of his arms, showing him. "I read the first three chapters of that book, and my heart sank, Arad, because I can't be that woman she talks about." She turned back around and looked out at her ocean.

"How did you get clean? I've heard it's one of the hardest things to overcome," he said, once more pulling her back into his arms.

She smiled. "I have a wonderful sponsor. To this day, Rue calls me every morning with a quote." She laughed. "You want to know what today's was?"

"Tell, my warrior's heart," he said and placed a kiss on the side of her neck, sending a chill up her spine.

"*It is during our darkest moments that we must focus to see the light*. This town was that light for me for the past three years. When my... I was married before, though we had a wonderful marriage, just had the twins when I found out he had three other ladies on the side. I filed for divorce, but someone told them about my past. I lost everything that day in court. All his friends there. I was lucky to get the photo albums of my babies."

She turned and looked up at him. "So, you see, wolf man, I am no warrior. Just a woman who lives day by day."

"Oh, but you are, Catarina. Every day you fight for your life, and you even took on three little children knowing that one day someone would come for them. You are the ultimate warrior fighting to stay in the light, but I'm here now to help you stay there. You will not be alone anymore, all mine," he said, reaching up and cupping her cheek.

The man smiled, and Catarina swore he was even more handsome. "What are you doing to me? How can I accept all off this?" she asked, stepping back, forgetting how close to the edge she was.

At once, Arad was there, grabbing onto her, bringing her back into his arms away from the edge. "Easy there; I've got you." He once more surrounded her with his arms. "The reason why you are accepting this is that it is the same reason I am." He rubbed her back. "Come here, little ones, we need to chat," he said, and that is when she noticed the three little ones behind them.

Arad moved her to the deck, pulling her down on the swing with him. The little ones sat across from them, watching. "We have to go back to put your mother to rest; she deserves this after all that was done to her. As you have heard, Catarina is my mate, so you will not be losing her. But you know Wolf and Trudy would love to have you live with them? The choice will be yours, this I give you after all that you have been through. Catarina, I would like you to come with us, meet my family. We can get to know each other better and decided where you would like to live."

She must have had her mouth hanging open when Arad reached over and whispered into her ear. "Breathe," he laughed.

Catarina looked up to see Ronnie and Frita standing there smiling at them.

"I thought something was up when you guys were in the diner," Frita said.

"Hush," Ronnie said. "I'm here with a proposal. This town has been running without an alpha for over a year. We need someone with your strength here. I've spoken with the bears, and they have even heard of you and what you have done for your people."

"Wow, you must be impressive. You sure you want to get saddled with me?" Catarina squeaked, and Arad growled.

"We are going to have to work on your self-doubt, all mine," he said, leaning over and nipping at her neck. "As for your offer, I thank you. We have a lot to consider, all of us, but first, we must send our loved ones to the next world. Can I give you an answer in two weeks?"

Ronnie bowed his head. "Even having you consider it is an honor. We will watch over your home, Catarina."

"I'll take over your classes to the children 'til you get back, but I know they will miss their teacher. Congrats, you both." Frita glanced at Arad. "Our Catarina is a very special woman, she deserved someone strong enough to help her. Maybe you can help get her little ones back, too." Frita growled. "Stupid, uptight..." She stopped, staring down at the children. "Sorry, but your babies should be with you."

"Thank you, but I don't want to stir up trouble, and we'd get a lot of it if we even went near that town. No, I won't risk anyone. Who knows, some of my father's men could be there. Nope, not going to happen." Catarina got up and hugged Frita. "Thank you."

"You deserve to be happy, too, Catarina. Every person does," Frita said as Catarina stepped back and bumped into Arad's chest.

"Again, thank you for the help. We'll stay in contact. I want to pull out tomorrow." Arad frowned. "We're going to need a trailer and an SUV.

"She has the SUV, and I have the trailer. I'll bring it down here tonight," Ronnie said. "You want me to put your bike on it?"

"Stop it, you just want to ride it," Frita said, nudging him with her elbow in the gut.

"You bet, anyone would want to ride it," the sheriff said, and Catarina couldn't help but laugh as Frita rolled her eyes.

Ronnie reached over and swatted Frita's ass. "Behave and don't think I didn't see that thing you do with your eyes."

"Here, have at it," Arad said, throwing Ronnie the keys. "And thank you again."

Catarina swore the man next to her was a walking sexbot. She thanked her friends again and made her way into the kitchen. Would she actually go with them to wherever he lived? Did she even risk stepping back in the States? She shook her head. "Risk is too high, but can I let the children go?"

* * *

Arad couldn't stop himself from touching her. Catarina was like a little, lost wolf. The sadness in her eyes alone had him wanting to just keep her at his side and not let go. If there were a way, he'd find a way to get her babies back for her.

But right now, hearing his mate talk to herself had him frowning. "What risk are you talking about?" Arad asked, coming inside.

She jumped and swung around. "Don't do that, you scared the living crap out of me." She grabbed her chest and took a deep breath and looked up at him. "Every time I enter the States, it's risky for me. It gives my father a heads-up that I'm close. Here in Canada, he does not have access to things, but in the States, he does." She looked behind him as the children came into the house. "I can't risk the children to go with you. What if he comes after you?"

He held out his hand. "Come here, all mine." Arad waited.

She looked at his hand then back at the children before stepping forward and sliding her hand into his. Arad knew she had done it because the children were there, but for now, he would take this. Soon, she won't hesitate, he'd make sure she trusted him and that he'd earn her trust.

"Do you really believe your father will be able to find you if you enter back in the States?" he asked and watch her nod.

"He always finds me, and the last time, my children were taken away. He helped Andrew with that." She looked down at the ground. "I don't want to risk the children."

Arad pulled out his phone and called his grandson Wolf. He knew he was working with the Ghost team now personally.

"*Trouble?*" Wolf answered on the second ring.

"There might be. I need you to contact your friend and have him check out a..."

"Otis Cruz, but it's not going to help. My father is like one of those lizard things," Catarina said and went to step away, but he held onto her.

"*On it. When will you be heading back?*" Wolf asked.

"Tomorrow, and I want this taken care of before we cross the border."

"*I'll call you back tonight, and congrats, Granddad If anyone deserves another love, it's you,*" Wolf said and disconnected the phone.

"We'll know more about the situation, but you know, officials don't usually put names in the database," Arad said.

"Normally, yes, but my father isn't normal, and I'm on the hot list. I found that out the hard way trying to get here," Catarina said. "I was lucky there was this lawyer there when the authorities pulled me into the station when I was trying to cross over, or who knows what my father would have done." She smiled. "That is when Barcus invited me here to Trinity Bay, and I haven't left yet. He's the town's attorney and a bear. We dated a few times, but my life was so screwed up, and well, I just wasn't ready then. Hell, I still don't know if I'm ready for all of this."

Arad snarled. "Is this bear still sniffing around?"

Catarina threw her head back and laughed. "You're jealous?" She shook her head and patted his chest.

His fingers twined with her one hand as he reached up and grabbed a handful of her thick blond hair. "I don't share, Catarina, never, and you are mine. If any male sniffs around you, they'll deal with me personally. You might want to admit it now, but you will be mine, all mine." He leaned down and nipped her bottom lip before placing a quick kiss on her lips and lifting his head.

Arad smiled at the confusion and passion in her gaze. His cock was hard to the point he thought for sure his jeans would rip open, but he enjoyed it. For the first time since his wife had died, he was alive inside.

Little hands tugged on his shirt as he glanced down to see Little Tee there staring up at him with her arms out.

Catarina sucked in her breath as he reached down and lifted his granddaughter. Catarina stared at each tiny hand on his cheeks. "Papa," she whispered and wrapped her arms around him.

"But..." he said as Marcus and Romy came to his side, staring up at him.

"We live with you two now. It's the first time

she's spoken since that night," Marcus said with tears in his eyes. "He hurt her worse than us."

"Well, now, I'm glad we have all this food from the diner. We can celebrate Little Tee's first word," Catarina said, leaning over and placing a kiss on her cheek. "Welcome back, Little Tee."

She spun around. "Marcus, pull out the sodas, one for each of us. This is a nice celebration. Romy, come help me get the paper plates, napkins, and silverware. Little Tee, why don't you run and get the blanket on the back of the couch."

"You know, it's clouding up outside, and the temps are dropping, why don't we have this picnic in front of the fireplace?" Arad asked.

Catarina glanced out the window and nodded. "Sounds like a plan. Could you move the coffee table out of the way for us? That will give us plenty of room to set up."

"Do you want me to start a fire?"

She shook her head. "I haven't had the money to get the chimney cleaned yet, that was next week's check."

Arad nodded and moved with Little Tee in his arms. "Come on, Little Tee, let's get this living room set up." He kissed her cheek, making a mental note to write out a list of things he wanted to be done to this house while they were gone.

If they came back here to live, he and Catarina would fix this place up, even though he was particular to log cabins. "Cedar," he said, putting Little Tee on the couch, grabbing the coffee table and setting it aside.

"What about cedar?" Catarina said.

"I was thinking the siding of this house would look nice with cedar."

She tilted her head to the side as if visioning it. "I never considered it because it was too expensive, but you are right, it would look wonderful."

"Good, then, while we are gone, I'll have cedar put up and the fireplace fixed. How is the roof?" he asked.

"What? You will not! We just met for Pete sakes. I'm not going to have you blowing thousands of dollars on me or my house." She glared at him, and he smiled.

"I'm doing this for us. I think we need to have a talk. Put the stuff down and come here," Arad said, sitting on the couch, waiting for her to come over to him.

She set the stuff on the floor and turned to move to the seat next to him, but he reached out and pulled her into his lap. His mate was round, her ass perfect to hold onto as he buried his cock into her, and her breasts full for his big hands to torture, play with.

"Has anyone explained the meaning of mates, bonding, and such?" he asked, waiting for her to relax.

"No, just figured it was like a wedding. Why? What am I missing?" Catarina asked and glanced at the children where Marcus and Romy were grinning. Little Tee was busy spreading the blanket out, concentrating hard on her task.

"I don't like the look of those grins. What do I not know?"

He smiled and leaned back. "Each species is different, but ours, we live a very long life. I'm still considered young, in my prime at the age of fifty-five. My father lived 'til he was three hundred and forty. We can marry as you humans do for love, as I did with my Starla, or if we are lucky enough, we find our bonded one, the one the Fates themselves has picked for us." He placed a kiss on her cheek. "And yes, the Fates are very real before you ask. You, Catarina, are my bonded one. The one the book you have in the kitchen was meant to find." He rubbed his chin on the top of her head.

"I don't know if this Delia has helped with her books or what. I know Wolf asked Delia's help to find his bonded one, and she did. I did not ask, so for Delia to have done this, well, I believe the Fate sisters are helping here. I, for one, will not throw this gift away."

Catarina stared at him. "Fates? Really? Wow. Wait, three hundred and forty?" her voice squeaked. "You're going to go through a lot of wives if they are human."

Marcus laughed, and Romy giggled.

"What?"

Arad couldn't help but laugh. "You are already changing, Catarina. Your life span will match mine, and soon, you will also have a wolf to call up."

Catarina jumped up and glared at him, pointing her finger at him. "Don't do that! I thought better..." Catarina spun and ran for her room, the door slamming shut a few seconds later.

"Marcus, what am I missing?" he asked, standing.

"I don't know? But she's crying, and it hurts," Marcus said.

"I know, it hurts me, too. Why don't you three get things all set up for our picnic, and I'll go apologize for whatever I said."

Chapter Four

Catarina curled up in the corner knowing she had overreacted, but when Arad had said something about having a wolf, she knew one of her dreams as a child was coming true. But would her father rip it away from her, too?

Remember, warrior woman: Every great dream begins with a dreamer. Always remember, you have within you the strength, the patience, and the passion to reach for the stars to change your world. Harriet Tubman said this, and it is so true for you.

Delia's words came back into her head again as if she were reading it. Catarina wiped the tears away, noticing Arad standing in front of her.

He reached down and lifted her into his arms as if she weighed nothing, carrying her over to the bed. Sitting down, he held her tight. "Tell me," he encouraged.

"Every time I dreamed of something, he would take it away. My dog, he killed it, shooting it with some drug. My children I always dreamed of having, he made sure they were taken away." Catarina looked up at him. "My father was obsessed with your kind. I think he was mad that you had longer lives while he would die. Anyway, as a child, I dreamed of being rescued by one of you. Taken away where he couldn't hurt me anymore. That I would be one of you, something he would never be."

Arad smiled down at her. "Well, you have your dream, so why so sad about it?" He placed a kiss on the top of her head. "He won't take you away from us, Catarina. I'll kill him first that I promise. Lean on me, all mine. I promise not to let you fall."

"You going to keep calling me *all mine*?" Catarina asked, taking a deep breath. He smelled so good.

"Yes, are you ready for our picnic? The children have it all set up waiting for us."

"Do you really think it's wise I go with you? The children are already getting so attached. What if one of their older siblings wants them to live with them? I don't want to stand in their way, and it will make it harder on the children."

He lifted her up and placed her in front of him, between his legs, holding onto her hips. "The children have already chosen, all mine. They want us to raise them, and right now, I think it's best we keep them close to you. They are still fighting the nightmares of what has happened, and you are their momma now, as I am their papa."

"I'll never replace her. What was done to that poor woman? Marcus explained a few things, but it was just so hard for him to speak of it." Catarina stepped back but held out her hand. "I can't promise I'm not going to flip out, so be pre-warned, wolf man, but I'm willing to try." She looked at the door.

"Your grandchildren mean the world to me, and there might be a small something starting to connect us," she teased.

He growled, standing and yanking her into his arms. Once more, his hand was in her hair and pulling her head back until she was staring into his beautiful eyes. "All mine," he said and covered her mouth, but this time, it wasn't a quick kiss.

Nope, wolf man was making love to her mouth, their tongues dancing like the wind and trees outside, in harmony and one, until his phone started to ring.

He lifted his head and growled. "I'm going to bite whoever interrupted us."

She patted his chest and laughed. "I have a feeling I'm going to get a lot of calls about you, wolf man, if you go biting everyone that gets in your way. Answer the phone and join us in the living room," she said as he pulled out the phone.

"Wait, it's Wolf; he might have news," Arad said, holding onto her as he answered the phone. "That was quick."

"Trouble?" she asked, hearing the little growls he was making as his grandson was speaking.

"Tell me why your father is so obsessed with you. Is there something more, all mine?" he asked.

"No, nothing that I know, that's why it's been so weird and scary." Arad leaned over kissing her.

"We'll figure it out. My grandson's friend and his team are going to meet us near Lewiston then we'll go from there."

"I still think it would be better for me to stay here," she mumbled.

"No, you don't leave my side," he told her, pulling her toward the door. "Together, we will figure out what is going on. Can I ask how long your father has been working with the government?"

"Before I was born, so I was told. Can we drop this subject? I really can't eat and speak of him at the same time. I really do get sick, it's like a natural reaction." She stopped in the hallway that entered into the living room. "You know what is really weird, I can't remember before I was six. Total blank. I don't know if I was abused before that or what, but yea. So, please, no talking about him?"

Arad wrapped both of his arms around her, hugging her tight. "We'll explore all of this together. You will never be alone, all mine." He smiled before leaning down and nipping her nose.

"Can I ask how long you and Starla were married?" Catarina felt him stiffen for a second but soon relaxed.

"Come, I'll tell all of you about Starla since the little ones don't remember her," Arad compromised.

"Good because they should remember her. She was a part of your lives, and Starla will always be alive in each of them, no matter what life journey she is on now." Catarina stopped and frowned. "Wow, where did all that come from?" She laughed.

"All mine, you are a very smart woman, and I can see why my grandchildren have chosen you to raise them." His hand slid down her to her butt, and he squeezed it. "But you really need to stop cutting yourself down, or I'm going to paddle this lovely butt."

"What?" she squeaked and glared up at him.

"You will not be hitting me."

"I don't hit women, but I do spank my woman if she puts herself in danger or does not listen to what is good for her." He lowered his head, his nose touching hers, and Catarina swore she could see the raw passion. If she were to admit it to herself, the idea of him spanking her... Well, she was actually wet now.

She stepped back but only a little because he wouldn't release her. "Not to worry, all mine, I can see what you need," he said, placing a quick kiss on her lips before Little Tee stepped between them, smiling up at them.

Her bright little smile warmed her heart. This little one had gone through so much and slowly was coming out of the shell she had built around her.

* * *

Arad sat back and watched as the children laughed and played the silly game *I Spy*. Something so old and simple had all three of his grandbabies happy, the fear he had seen in their eyes gone at least for this time frame.

"I see a big blob," Catarina said, drawing him out of his thoughts.

"What kind of a description is that?" he asked.

"Grandpa," Romy laughed, and Catarina nodded.

"You called me a blob?" Arad growled.

"Well, you were sitting there daydreaming like a blob," Catarina said, inching away from him.

"Marcus, now would be a good time to practice that sneaky thing you were doing with the bears yesterday."

Arad turned his gaze on his grandson, who laughed. "Not a chance," Marcus laughed, backing up as Arad jumped up and grabbed onto to Catarina before she could flee.

"So not fair," she squealed as he sat back down with her in his arms, nipping at her neck.

"I don't play fair when it comes to my family," he said, sucking part of her skin into his mouth, knowing he'd leave a nice sucker bite on her.

"Arad, we're not teenagers," she laughed and tried to pull away, but he held on for a few seconds longer before releasing her, placing a kiss on the spot. "All mine," he stated and glanced over at Marcus.

"So, you were learning to stalk yesterday?" he asked Marcus.

"Sheriff Ronnie showed me a few moves when we first got here, and I've been practicing them with the bears."

"Marcus, you do know bears don't stalk as we do in our other form, right?" he asked, and the boy laughed, almost falling over.

"I tried to tell that to Stanley, but he kept trying," Marcus said.

"Stanley is the little boy next door, Marcus's age. Actually, there are three boys and two girls. Stanley, Trish, Caleb, Eddy, and Suzy, she's Little Tee's age. Thea is an amazing woman, raising five little ones all by herself. Her mate was shot last winter, it was the saddest thing. I didn't think the children would ever heal," Catarina said, rubbing her cheek on his chest.

"I have the kids over for breakfast two mornings a week, so Thea can go to work early. I get them all off to school except for Suzy, she stays here with me." Catarina sat up, frowning. "Can I borrow your phone. I need to call Thea and let her know we won't be here next week."

Arad handed her the phone and frowned. This city needed a lot of help. One thing was for sure, a mother raising children alone would always be looked after. He looked up, hearing a truck pull up.

Lifting Catarina up, Arad went to meet the sheriff, wanting to speak with him, but when he looked down, Arad noticed he had a shadow, Marcus.

Arad didn't say anything, allowing him to come with him. In so many ways, Marcus was as his older brother was at this age. He smiled, remembering Wolf following him around the pack, checking on daily issues.

Arad stepped outside, taking in the scene and the scents. "Always check your area before you move out into the open. Never leave yourself open, unless it is necessary."

Ronnie moved around the corner and smiled. "Your grandson is a quick study, and now that he has you, he'll be just as powerful as you are someday."

"Thank you. I wanted to speak to you about a few things while we are gone." All three of them moved to the trailer as he discussed what he would like done while he was gone.

Before long, Catarina and the girls were coming

out to join them. Little Tee in Catarina's arms and Romy holding onto her other hand. Never had anyone looked so stunning to him. He loved his wife, but this bonding was so different, and Arad could actually understand how connected a couple becomes.

He almost felt a little cheated as Arad and Starla never had this before, but then again, it wouldn't have been with Catarina. "Here, let me take Little Tee," he said, reaching over and taking the little bundle, knowing she could get a little heavy after a while.

"Ronnie is going to take care of a few things for me while we are away. Did you contact your friend?" he asked.

"Yes, and Frita had already volunteered to help out for the next week, so we are all set, even though Stanley was very disappointed he wouldn't have Marcus to help him train," Catarina said.

"Hmm, Marcus, why don't you go get Stanley. I can show you both some things to work on this week while we are gone. I'm sure Ronnie will check on Stanley while we are gone, too."

"I have no problem with that, but you really should take some men with you, traveling with the children," Ronnie said.

Arad turned toward the hill overlooking the city and smiled. "Marcus, what do you scent?" he asked as Ronnie glanced up at the hill.

The boy turned and took a deep breath before he smiled. "Bryon and Marty are here?" he asked, and Arad nodded.

"Even though I'm going to thump your brother

Wolf for risking his brothers, but then again, they aren't alone, at least." Arad frowned when Little Tee squirmed in his arms until he let her go.

Little Tee ran for Catarina, burying her face into her leg. "Hey, what's wrong, baby?" Catarina knelt down and was almost knocked over by Little Tee's reaction, jumping into her arms.

"She's afraid of them. They smell like him," Marcus said, reaching over and running his hand over Little Tee's back.

Catarina glanced up at him. "If she is going to do this to two of her brothers, how is she going to handle the others?" Catarina asked, standing as she watched Bryon and Marty come down the road with ten other men following them.

"We'll have to work with her, but she'll always have us there with her." Arad moved to Catarina's side. "Little Tee, we are not going to leave you, and I promise to help protect you, little one. Your brothers would, too." He leaned over and kissed the top of her head.

"I guess that answers my question about who's going to help you," Ronnie said, moving to the end of the drive.

"Yes, but it's also going to draw more attention to us if we stick together," Arad said. "Why don't you take the girls back inside; we'll be in in a minute," Arad said as his grandsons Marty and Bryon both met his gaze before moving it to Catarina, and he didn't like it one bit. "Go on now," he said, pushing her toward the door, glancing over at the two, baring his teeth.

"Arad, are you okay?" Catarina asked, already

picking up his distress.

"Just getting a little protective, all mine. Please, go inside while I speak with my grandsons and the others. It will help me calm knowing you are safe inside," he encouraged her.

She smiled and shook her head. "Silly wolves," she said to Little Tee and Romy.

One day, Catarina would understand how deadly this kind of situation could get, especially since they were still bonding. As soon as the door closed, Marty and Bryon stepped up behind him.

"I am very close to ripping your hearts out, don't push it, boys, and why the hell did you come? You know it will draw attention to have all of us around," Arad asked.

Marty got all serious. "From what Wolf's friend, the CIA guy, said, this guy, her father, is not all there. He has gone crazy the last few years looking for her, knowing he couldn't cross the border, that he'd be arrested on the spot. Seems he did a little experimenting up here in the mountains." Marty glanced at the door. "He was experimenting on a little girl. One that had been taken from a family when she was an infant."

Everything in him froze. "What family? What kind of experiments?" Arad snarled as did Marcus, drawing his attention.

Both Byron and Marty knelt down, but Marcus stepped back, snarling. Catarina had been right, it was going to take all three children a long time to get over what had happened to them. "Marcus, look at me, son," Arad said, placing a hand on his shoulder, waiting.

A few minutes later, Marcus looked up at him. "They are your brothers and will not hurt you, Marcus. They are not infected or even close to what he was like. You know this, remember." Arad and the others waited.

Marcus relaxed a little but also inched closer to Arad, and he sighed. "I'm afraid it's worse with the girls. My mate, Catarina, has done a wonderful job with the little ones, but what they have experienced will take some time. All of them have already formed a bond with Catarina and won't let it go."

"You're going to raise them?" Marty asked, standing.

"Yes, we just haven't decided where we are going to live, but if what you say is true, we'll most likely spend the next few years here. Do you have the report? I want to give it to Ronnie, he can do some digging while we are away and see if he can see if Catarina is this missing girl. I can see why he didn't want her here if it is true."

"Are you going to inform her?" Bryon asked.

Arad reached over and squeezed Bryon's shoulder. "Yes, there should never be lies between a man and his woman. Bryon, if I could have stopped your father, if I would have known what he did to you and the little ones..."

Bryon shook his head. "No, it's no one's fault. I shouldn't have left myself open, but then again, I didn't think he'd do what he did either." Bryon glanced down at Marcus. "I guess we were all hurt by him, no?"

"Marcus, why don't you go get Stanley. We can

even see if your brothers remember their training here in a few minutes," Arad said, earning a frown from Marty as he dug out some papers.

"Okay, old man, what do you have up your sleeve? If I remember right, you always had us on the ground in seconds. I only have one copy of this." Marty grumbled, and he laughed as Marcus ran off to get his friend.

"You shall see, and the little boy he is getting is his friend, a bear, his father was shot and killed. I believe I saw a copy machine inside," Arad said, glancing over his shoulder at his grandsons, warning them to tread lightly around the young ones. Now the real test, how well he was going to handle males around his woman.

Chapter Five

Catarina sat on the couch, watching as Arad's grandson Marty used her copy machine. But she still couldn't get over how each of the men looked like Arad.

"Stop staring," Arad growled and nipped her neck, sitting next to her as they waited for Marcus to get back with Stanley.

"It's just weird. They look so much like you. You could be their father. You must have some strong little buggers there," she said before censoring her words. All eyes turned to her. "Well crap, sorry, just used to saying what I'm thinking." Catarina smiled.

"We're here," Marcus yelled as he came in with Stanley and his mom, Thea.

"Wow, full house, and damn girl, they are all big," Thea said, coming over, giving her a hug along with Little Tee, who still clung to Catarina's neck with her brothers around.

Thea frowned and shook her head. "It's going to take a long time for this one, I think. Little Tee, Suzy is out back with Trish. You want to go play with them?" Thea asked right before she lifted her head and sniffed, turning and looking toward Marty, who was now staring at Thea, too.

Catarina looked up at Arad, who was also watching.

"Marty?" Arad asked.

Marty smiled. "Guess I don't need a book. It would seem you are not the only one who will be staying around, old man."

"Well crap, I knew there was a possibility of finding another, but damn," Thea said and looked at Catarina. "Mate," Thea whispered the last part to Catarina.

"Wow, okay. Well, then, I'm happy for you, I think. But be warned." Catarina leaned over and whispered, "If he is anything like his grandfather, they are a stubborn lot."

Arad snorted behind her and smacked her ass as he started to herd the boys outside. "Yep, going to have to make a paddle."

"You will not," Catarina said, following him as everyone else did. "And that hurt," she growled, which had Little Tee lifting her head up and staring at her. Arad turned to look at her, too.

"Easy there, Little Tee, I'm just playing with your grandpa as he was playing with me," Catarina comforted, trying to reassure the child but wondering why the hell she just growled.

"Catarina." Arad came up to her wrapped his arm around her waist. "Close your eyes and look inside. Tell me what you see."

"Why?" she asked, leery at the way everyone was looking at her. Well, at least Marty and Thea weren't, they were too busy staring and sniffing each other.

"All mine, now," Arad ordered.

"You are also very bossy," she grumbled, doing what he asked, but what she saw had her popping her eyes back open as her legs threatened to give out.

His grasped around her neck, holding her as her gaze met his.

"How can this be? We just met, and why does my wolf look deformed, it had fangs." She glared at him. "Wait," Catarina held up her hand and took a deep breath. Her heart seemed to be in her throat. "He, my father, did something to me, didn't he?"

Little Tee's arms tightened around Catarina's neck, and she glanced down at her, rubbing her back. "I'm okay, Little Tee. I'll be fine, I promise. Why don't you go play with Suzy? Remember, you are safe here, no one is going to hurt you. I won't let them, I promise."

Catarina lowered Little Tee down, placing a kiss on the top of her head. "Promise," she repeated.

At first, Little Tee glanced at Suzy, who came running up to her, then back to Catarina. "Go on, I'm not going anywhere. I'll be right out here with you and so will your grandpa." Catarina pushed Little Tee toward Suzy, who took her hand and pulled her toward the big sandbox Catarina had put in last month for the girls.

"How bad did my father screw with me? Am I even his daughter?" Catarina asked, straightening up and turning to the handsome, hot man behind her, her mate he had called her.

Arad pulled her into his arms. "We're not sure. There are reports coming in, but I want everything checked out before I say anything, Catarina. There is no sense in getting upset until we know the truth. But if I had to guess, yes, your father did something to you. One day at a time, Catarina. I have a feeling that is also why he wants to know where you are."

She grabbed onto Arad. "Oh my god, Arad, what about my little girls? If I'm like you guys, will my girls be like me, too? Would he come after them?" Catarina shook at the thought of that man near her little babies.

Arad hugged her tight. "I don't know, but I want you to write down the city and your old address. I'll have Wolf send people there to watch the children 'til we can get there to collect your babies."

She shook her head. "My ex isn't going to allow us to take the girls no matter what. What a freak cluster..." Catarina looked down to see Marcus there with Stanley.

"We'll help get them back," Marcus said, and tears filled her eyes.

"Thank you. Now, I do believe you two are waiting for some kind of lesson?" She looked up at Arad.

"Byron, you're the guinea pig right now since your brother can't stop sniffing his mate," Arad called out, moving to the middle of the yard, waiting for Bryon to step out.

"You know, I really hate this," Bryon mumbled. "Marcus, you better appreciate this, because next time, it's going to be your butt on the ground."

Catarina never laughed so hard watching Bryon and Marcus trying to throw Arad onto the ground that she didn't see Arad sneak up to her and swing her up into his arms.

"What are you laughing at, all mine?" He

snarled and bit down on her shoulder.

"Hey, stop that." She tried to push his head away, but all she got was another growl. "Fine, I was laughing because I couldn't believe two young men couldn't take down their grandfather. Hell, even the boys were in awe of you, wolf man." Catarina tapped his arm and nodded to Marcus and Stanley.

"Look at how much you have already impressed the boys." Catarina smiled and held back the laugh as Stanley fell face first in the mud.

"My poor boy," Thea laughed, moving next to them. "Thank you for including him. He is bound and determined to be able to protect me since his father was killed."

"Both my grandfather and I will work with him, and nothing is going to happen to you," Marty grumbled, walking up to them as he tried to brush off his pants. "Now, I look and smell like a warthog." He looked up and glared at Arad, who snorted.

"You're getting lazy, Marty. The both of you have forgotten what I tried to teach you so long ago," Arad said, lowering Catarina's feet down but holding onto her.

"Hey, that's a little harsh," Catarina said, shoving her elbow back into Arad's gut but only ended up hurting her damn elbow. "What are you, stone?" she grumbled and rubbed her elbow, glaring at him.

"He's right." Marty smiled. "The only one that actually kept up with the training and such was Wolf. Now, I'd like to see you and Wolf go at it."

Marty smiled, and Bryon snorted.

"I hate to say it, but I put bets on Wolf; he's old," Bryon said, earning a swat upside the back of his head.

"Watch it, boy, this old wolf can take you down in nothing flat," Arad said. "The sheriff is coming. I want you to give him a copy of that report. While we are away, he can start digging on this end while Wolf's men dig in States," Arad order, and at once, his grandsons straightened and moved toward the driveway.

"You stay here with the children, please," Arad said, placing a kiss on her cheek before following his grandsons.

Thea must have seen confusion on Catarina's face as she moved around, getting a look at the drive. "Get used to it. Anytime strangers are around a male's mate, there is caution, and with the alpha there, they are going to be three times worse. Any threat to you or the children and all hell will break loose." Thea bumped Catarina's hip. "Welcome to my world, Grandma," she teased.

"What?" Catarina laughed. "I guess I am a grandma, but it's weird, too, if that is the case. I mean, aren't Marty and Byron older than me? But then again, who knows how old I really am, too." She shook her head. "This really sucks not knowing. God, I hate that man."

"Who? Your so-called father or your ex?" Thea asked as the little girls came over to them.

"We're hungry," Suzy said, and Little Tea nodded. Behind them were Marcus, Stanley, and Romy with Thea's other children.

"Well, we didn't get to eat yet, so Marcus, you and Stanley go clean up. Thea, why don't you and the kids stay and have dinner with us since it's obvious you are going to be family anyway."

"I have fried chicken, potato salad, and dessert. The kids and I will bring it over." Thea ushered her group off to collect the food and stuff as Catarina moved into the house with her three.

"So weird."

"What's weird?" Marcus asked.

"Nothing, just thinking out loud. Go, clean up now and make sure to clean the tub when you're done, and yes, that means a shower to, Marcus." She stared down at him, and he smiled.

"I'm glad you're going to be our mom," he said before disappearing down the hall.

"Well, shit," Catarina slipped. At once, both Romy and Little Tee looked at her, surprised. "Sorry, little ones, just been a long day. Come on, let's push this couch back to give us some more room."

* * *

Arad stared at Catarina, smiling as Marcus and the young ones tackled her and brought her down to the ground. *"Well, Starla, I've found my mate, I hope like hell you have found yours in the next life. I still miss you, but for the first time, there is peace. I promise to take care of our grandchildren,"* he said before going in and rescuing his woman.

"It's about time you got here. I thought you were going to stand there looking goofy all day,"

Catarina laughed.

He frowned. "You know, maybe the children have it right, and you need to be tickled. I did not have a goofy face," he said before diving into the pile and tickling Catarina.

"She was right though you did have a goofy look on your face," Marcus said, jumping up ready to bolt, but Arad was quicker grabbing Marcus around the waist and throwing him up in the air.

"I'll give you goofy," he grumbled but couldn't help but laugh as the two little girls attacked his legs, but he was saved when Thea and her children came in carrying trays of food.

"She cooks for an army, but then again, Thea has her own little army," Catarina said, coming to stand next to him. "So, what did the sheriff have to say? Had he heard anything about my father?"

"Sorry, no, all mine. But he heard of the story and is going to do some digging for us." Arad heard the sigh.

"I guess it doesn't matter really, it is what it is. Let's join the others," Catarina said and stepped away from him, but he pulled her back into his arms.

"You know, no matter what you are, you are mine? I'm not going to let you go, Catarina, so get used to being in my arms. When you said earlier I was bossy, honey, you have no idea yet." He kissed the top of her nose.

"I have decided I'm going to go with you guys tomorrow," Thea announced as Arad and Catarina joined the others. "I've already talked with Frita. The children will be staying with them 'til we return."

"You will not!" Marty growled, moving to Thea. "You know how dangerous this is going to be?"

Thea pulled back and glared at Marty. "I'm going. I want to meet the rest of your family, and I will be there for you to bury your mother. Plus, Catarina needs someone there for her, and I'm not letting her do it alone. So, back off, wolf," she snarled, and Arad could see the bear rise up as everyone stared at them.

"We would welcome you, and Catarina would love the company, but if you come, Thea, you will listen to every word we say. There will not be an exception," Arad said.

Marty looked up at Arad, growling, and he held up his hand. "You would be worried sick about her being here since you haven't finished the bonding. This is the best solution, plus you can pick up a paddle on the way back. I saw this nice place I do believe we are going to have to visit."

Catarina stepped back and glared up at him. "Keep threating, wolf man, and you'll have that paddle upside your damn head," she said as the sheriff and his wife walked into the room. All eyes were on them, she had just confronted the alpha in the room, and his wolf was itching to show her.

"All mine," he whispered, lifting her up and over his shoulder, swatting her ass. "Excuse me. I have to speak with my woman for a second. Please, start eating; we'll be right back," Arad said and moved to her bedroom as she tried to get down, growling at him.

"Damn it, Arad, put me down now!" Catarina

demanded.

He sat on the bed, swinging her around, so she lay across his lap. "You are lucky I just met you because I will not stand to be confronted in front of others. Is that understood?" His hand came down on her ass hard. "Our lives are dangerous, and everyone must work together." He slapped her three more times as she tried to get away, and that is when Catarina bit his leg.

Arad was so shocked, he stared down at his little hellfire and smiled. "Oh, all mine, we are going to burn up the sheets."

Catarina was wet, and if he wasn't mistaken, she was also close to her cycle, and the thought of her carrying his pup inside her had him stripping her clothes in seconds before backing her up against the closed door.

He pushed his hand between her legs, and he had been right. Sliding two fingers into her pussy, she snarled and tried to get away. "Don't!" he snarled. "Look at me," Arad ordered, and at once, her gaze met his.

"Take a deep breath, Catarina. I don't know how, but your wolf is pushing us to mate here and now," Arad said, leaning down and sucking her rose-colored nipple into his mouth.

"I need... What is wrong? I'm burning up; stop it, please," Catarina pleaded, her arms grabbing onto his shoulders as she rode his fingers up and down.

"If I take you now, you'll most likely carry my child after tonight, Catarina. There is no mistaking you are ready to breed," he said, releasing her nipple.

All struggling stopped, and tears filled her eyes. "They'll take it away. All my children will go away."

"Never! They'll have to kill me first. No one is going to take our children, all mine, no one," Arad promised as she started again to fuck herself.

"I hurt, so confused." She laid her forehead against his. "Take me, Arad, and god help you if you betray me." Catarina gave herself to him, and Arad didn't waste time releasing his cock and burying it where his fingers had been.

Arad had heard of mates coming together hot and heavy. That a true female alpha would test her male, making him take control, testing him, and he wasn't about to back down. She was his, and everyone would know when he got done loving and claiming her.

All thought of the others in the living room left, knowing his grandsons would watch over the little ones. His only worries were how Catarina would feel after he claimed, loved her. He reached around her, lifting her up by the ass cheeks, squeezing them, knowing his woman craved the pain he could give her.

He hadn't been wrong. She buried her nails into his shoulders and snarled, which brought out his wolf. Their loving became rough, hard, and quick as he spanked and bit down on her shoulder, holding her as he loved her.

Her pussy squeezing his cock, her little snarls, and at the end, her whimpers were all it took. Both of them shook in each other's arms, his pants now at his feet. Arad released her shoulder, licking and placing a kiss on it, his seed buried deep inside her.

That night, they had created a little life, Arad could feel it down to his soul. "You, my little mate, are perfect, but be warned. Next time you confront me in front of guests, there will be no other room. I will spank your butt right there and then," Arad promised, pulling back a little to stare down at her passion-filled eyes.

"Hmm, why does it mean so much? I was only playing, well part of it, at least." She lifted her head and stared at him. "We're married now, aren't we? In your world."

He hated to, but Arad pulled out of her, moaning. "Yes, but it's more than the marriage of the humans. Since you are my mate and I claimed you the old fashion way, if you die, I die too and vice versa. As for what happened out there earlier. In this little town, there is no alpha. I am or was one of the most powerful men in our world, and no, I'm not saying that to brag." He reached down and pulled up his pants, tucking his still semi-hard cock into his pants and zipped them up before leading her back to the bed.

Pulling her in-between his legs, he stared up at her. "You will respect me in front of others, all mine. The alpha is always being judged by others. If I appear weak at any time, someone could challenge me or seek to hurt you. I promise, I'll share all that I know, but this is the most important thing I must ask of you, even if you were just playing."

Chapter Six

Oh my god, she was married, and Catarina had only known the man a few freaking hours. "I'm a damn slut," she muttered but jumped when said man slapped her ass hard, glaring at her.

"I don't want to hear that come out of your mouth again," Arad snarled and pulled her down onto his lap, and she flinched, her butt burning from his spanking earlier.

"Ouch, that hurt," she grumbled and glared back. "And I can call myself anything I want. But come on, who else would marry and fuck a man she'd only known for a few hours?"

Arad grabbed onto a handful of her hair and pulled her head back, his nose now touching hers. "We are not human! Our world is totally different from the human world. We did not fuck, I claimed my woman, loved her as she needed me." He nipped her bottom lip. "Tell me what you feel in your heart, all mine. Really look deep. Do you want me to leave?" he asked, releasing her.

Catarina frowned, the instant he said the words asking if she wanted him to leave, she swore her heart stopped beating, and emptiness so big settled over her. Tears filled her eyes, not understanding the emotions running through her right now.

"Oh, all mine, I'm sorry." Arad pulled her into a

tight hug. "I'm not leaving, Catarina. Someone would have to kill me. You are part of me now, all mine." He kissed the top of her head, holding her.

"All of this is so confusing. I'm sorry if I embarrassed you earlier. I still can't believe... I mean, I've never had sex like that." Catarina went to jump up, but he held onto her.

"Relax; no one will come in this room, and I happen to like you this way in my lap so I can touch you." He reached over and cupped her breast. "You are so beautiful, but you are right. We have a house full of guests." Arad lifted her up, releasing her.

"Where are my clothes?" She reached down and lifted her sweater, which was ripped in half. "Wow, you're a strong one, aren't you?" Catarina once more stared at the man sitting on her bed, until she heard his growl. Her gaze met his.

"You keep staring at me like that and we won't be going anywhere, company be damned. Get dressed, all mine." He reached down and grabbed his shirt, putting it on, but his gaze watched her every move as she pulled out a different outfit, this time making sure it was old just in case her man decided to make mincemeat of her clothes again. From the look on his face, she would be lucky if they made it out of the bedroom.

"Stop that, the children are waiting for us," she mumbled, pulling her old T-shirt over her head, forgetting the bra. She'd be damn if he ripped another one of those up since it cost her an arm and a leg to purchase them in her size. Catarina would just wear her sweater over her.

Arad came up behind her, reaching around, sliding his hands under her shirt, cupping her breasts. "Is there a reason you're not wearing a bra? I mean, I like that I have free access, but the thought of others..." He snarled in her ear before biting down on her neck.

"Hey, that hurts, and yes, I can't afford any new bras right now. When you are big, you have to order them, and those suckers cost a pretty penny." She turned and looked up at him. "And you, dear wolf man, just shredded my new one."

"Well then, I'll have to buy you more now, won't I? Now, come on, let's get moving before I do it again." He placed a quick, hard kiss on her before he was pulling her through the door.

In the family room, all eyes turned them. His older grandsons whistled, and the three little ones came running, hugging her. She glanced up at him, frowning. "They know? How?" she asked.

Thea laughed and came over, pulling her into the room. "Sweetie, his scent is all over you, and he's also marked you. The minute you walked out of that room, everyone knew you were mated."

She pulled out her shirt and sniffed. "I stink? Do I need to take a shower?" Catarina asked, and Arad laughed behind her.

"Not that kind of scent. Our scents have mixed, there is no more just Catarina or Arad, there is now us," he explained. "Sit; you need to eat. It's been a long day, and with your animal coming on strong, you are going to need to make sure to eat a lot of protein."

"Protein, you're talking about meat, aren't you?"

She sat down as Thea handed her a plate and started to pile the food on it.

"Yes, he is. When your first change is upon you, believe me, it wipes you out." Thea frowned. "You should shift before we leave, that way you'll know what to expect, and if there is trouble, you can change faster. Don't you think so, Alpha?" Thea asked, looking at Arad as he sat down next to Catarina on the floor.

"That is a smart idea. Maybe tonight we can go for a run, take the little ones with us," Arad said, earning smiles from all three of them.

"Never was into running much. Well, until I found out psycho Dad was trying to get me." She took a bite of the casserole and moaned. "I tell you what, Rose can cook. Taste this." She got another heaping on her fork and held it to Arad's mouth.

He took the bite, but the room had gotten quiet again. She sighed and looked around the room. "Okay, what did I do wrong now?" she asked. "If this keeps up, I'm going to get a damn complex here."

Arad snorted and pulled her into his lap, putting his plate down. "It's nothing bad. Matter of fact, it's good. It shows the others that you care for your man, your alpha. That like I will take care of you, you will take care of me. In other words, you honored me," he said.

"Oh, okay. Now, let me go so you can eat."

"Give me a kiss first, all mine."

She laughed and leaned in, planning to give him a quick kiss, but this was not a quick kiss. If kisses had a Richter scale, then Arad just planted a number ten on her.

"Wow," Catarina said, touching her finger to her lips. "Damn, you're good at that."

The room exploded with laughs all around, and Catarina swore her face turned a bright red as heat rose up and she slid off his lap. "I swear, I'll learn yet to keep my mouth shut," she mumbled and snorted, knowing that wouldn't happen anytime soon.

Little Tee crawled onto her lap, resting her head against her chest. "Momma," she said, hugging her tight.

A lump formed in Catarina's throat as she placed a kiss on the top of Little Tee's head.

Romy scooted to the other side of her as Marcus sat in front of them. Arad's grandsons Bryon and Marcus sat across them, watching their siblings, frowning.

"They really have formed a bond with her," Byron said as he stuffed a bite of the casserole into his mouth. "Never heard of anything like it, have you, Marty?"

Arad growled, and she jumped. "You really need to stop that. Now, why are you upset?" she asked.

"Byron, quit staring at my woman, and it's happened before. From what I have found out when our children experience something so horrific, it's like they are lost. Catarina was the first light that all three children had that didn't disappear and stayed with them." Arad wrapped his arm around her and pulled her and Little Tee closer.

"Ronnie, I want constant reports if you find anything about that little girl while we are gone. I don't want surprises. Also, I want a list of who live in the city and outer areas. Frita, when you have time, if you could compile a list of homes that need working on."

Catarina listened half on and half off, wondering if it were true that she had been taken from her parents. It would explain so much, but what had he done to her? She took a bite of her food when she heard some giggling and looked down to see Little Tee laughing with a piece of beef on the top of her head.

She laughed. "Sorry, baby. Guess I was thinking too hard," Catarina said.

"Were you thinking of that little girl that was taken?" Romy asked.

"You, my dear, are a smart one." Catarina poked Romy's nose with her fork, and she smiled. "And yes, how can I not. I mean, maybe I have some good family out there."

"Well, you have a good family here, too," Thea said, looking at her. "All of us consider you part of our family now, Catarina. We have for a while."

"Okay, stop it." Catarina wiped the tear that slid down her cheek. "I hate when I cry," she mumbled, waving her fork at Thea, who only laughed. Arad leaned over and placed a kiss on the top of her head, rubbing her arm.

* * *

Arad shook Ronnie's hand and stepped back next to Catarina as the sheriff left with his wife. He'd wanted to come with them on their first run here, saying the alpha should have protection, but he had enough protection with his grandsons and the group that they brought.

He looked over his shoulder. "We'll be back in a minute," he told his grandsons and lead a nervous Catarina to the back yard.

"What if I can't do this? Or I'm a freak? You never know what he did to me," she worried, looking up at Arad as he turned her to face him.

"You're not going to be a freak. You might be different, but we all are. Now, are you ready?" he asked, and she sighed, nodding.

"I'm going help you, but I want you to let go, release yourself to the animal inside you. You are safe, Catarina. No one is going to hurt you," he said, and Arad meant every word. He'd kill anyone who tried to harm his woman.

She whimpered, drawing Marcus forward, but Arad shook his head. "She's got this, Marcus, it's just the unknown that has her scared." Arad tried to reassure the children as he watched his woman shift. A process that shouldn't have taken as long as it did, but what stood before him even had him stunned.

Arad walked around the stunning little wolf, but she was more. If he wasn't mistaken, his mate also had part bear and vampire. Would this first shift bring on the thirst? He'd have to watch her and find his old friend to help him. Because Arad knew the first drink was an important one.

He stopped in front of her and knelt down. "You are stunning, all mine. I believe you are part bear, wolf, and vampire. You are going to be very strong, a perfect mate for an alpha," he said, and Arad swore the wolf rolled its eyes at him.

"All mine," he growled. At once, her wolf went to the ground, and he smiled. "Good. Little ones, shift; it's time we went for a run," Arad said, shifting and watching Little Tee, making sure she was all right as she shifted.

Little pups sometimes had trouble, but his granddaughter did him proud as he moved in front of his family, heading to his grandsons. Behind him, Catarina stayed with the children, watching.

Even though Catarina didn't know the hierarchy, she still made sure the children were protected. At once, both Bryon and Marty turned and stared at Catarina as they came around the corner.

Arad snarled. *"Stop it; she's already nervous enough. Let's get moving. I want to know the land around the city, and it's going to take us a little while with the little ones."*

At once, his grandsons shifted. Thea and her children came around the corner all changed into their bear form. Marty moved toward Thea, sniffing around her, licking her fur before he pushed her toward Catarina and the children.

All the males surrounded their group as they made their way into the hills. Arad did have to admit the place was beautiful even in the evening, but hearing a whine, Arad spun around, and his heart sank as Catarina went down, a small red splotch appearing on her shoulder. His mate had been shot. He shifted, going toward her.

The children ran toward their Catarina at once, forming a circle around her, as did Thea and her children. Each one of them ready and waiting as his men and grandsons moved out searching for the one that shot her.

"I have her, Alpha. It's a shoulder hit. Find the bastard that has done this," Thea growled.

Never had he been more torn right there until his woman looked up at him. "I'm fine, get the bastard, please. They could have shot one of the children," she growled.

He smiled and nodded. "Get them home, and all mine," he said, "I'm proud of you. Turtle, Frank, Thomas, escort my family home and don't leave them. Call in the sheriff when you get there. If we have someone taking pot shots, I want all the women and children inside now," he ordered and shifted into a form only the strongest could make.

Running toward where his grandsons had taken off to, Arad let off a howl that echoed in the hills surrounding them. He stood over nine-feet tall, and in his beast form, he could run faster than his wolf form, plus twice as deadly.

The person who shot his mate better be miles away from here. The anger and need to destroy anyone that would hurt her was the only thing he was thinking as he weaved in and out of the trees, making sure he wasn't an easy target for whoever shot at them. That's when he heard it and dived to the ground, rolling as another round of fire went off.

"Really, Grandfather, you must be getting old," Marty sent as Arad picked up the stranger's scent coming from the North.

"I really did expect more, but then, you are

smitten with a certain pretty female back there," Byron teased, coming in from the west.

"Bryon, you don't need to be looking at my mate, and the both of you, shut up." He snarled at himself for not seeing the signs, which only made him more furious. One, Arad was out of form, and that would change now that he had a ready-made family. Two, he was going to make an example of said shooter, because this was no hunter.

Chapter Seven

*C*atarina was furious. Not only was her shoulder hurting like a bitch after the doc showed up and dug out the bullet, but the thought of the children in the line of fire... Now, Arad was out there with his grandsons and a few others, and god knew what was happening to them.

"Alpha Catarina, please come sit. You pacing is not going to help with healing the wound," the doc said, staring at her.

She grumbled and sat down as he requested, but Catarina had to admit she was having a very hard time doing that. "Is this normal? I can't just sit here." She growled and got back up to pace again.

The doc stepped in front of her, and at once, Catarina jumped back, hissing. That is when she noticed the fangs as her tongue scraped one of them. "What the hell?" She ran to the mirror and moaned. "Of courth, thomething elth hath to happen. It'th not enough I was thot at, no."

"Frita, call..." Doc Sam was about to say something when a very, very tall, thin man stepped into the living room.

The children ran to her as Arad's guards moved around her, growling. "Who is this?" Turtle asked.

"Easy, everyone. This is the man I was going to have Frita call, and Gunner, if you don't stop scaring the kids, I'm going to rip your skinny ass apart." Doc grunted, taking a deep breath. "You know why I was going to call you?" Doc asked, and the man nodded.

"I could feel the need. I got here as fast as I could. I'm just surprised she hasn't had the first feeding before now," Gunner said, and that is when Catarina noticed his fangs as he spoke.

"Doc, what's going on?" Catarina asked at the same time seeing if her wolf man could hear her. "*I know you are probably kind of busy right now, wolf man, but I'm about to flip out here. There is a fanged man in my living room,*" she said, leaning down and taking Little Tee into her arms as Romy wrapped her arms around her waist and Marcus stepped in front of her, snarling.

"Relax, Marcus, I know this old geezer, and he will not hurt anyone here," Arad said, coming over and taking Little Tee out of her arms. "You need to heal first before you lift anyone up." Arad nodded to her shoulder. "You've opened the wound again."

She shrugged. "They needed me, and I'm not going to deny them. Why is he here?" she asked, moving in closer to Arad.

"As the doc here has said, this is Gunner. The last I heard, you were in Europe."

"No, too much political crap." Gunner nodded to her. "I take it this is your mate?"

"She is, and why do you keep staring at her?" Arad snarled, and his friend held up his hands.

"I'm afraid your woman is going to need her first drink. I could feel the call from my home," Gunner informed them.

Arad moved until he was standing in front of her. "All mine, look at me."

She frowned and looked up at him. "What's going on, and what is first drink? Or do I even want to know?"

"She has calmed since you came into the room, but you know this will not last," Gunner said, now behind Arad.

Catarina couldn't help but step back. Up close, Gunner was impressive and a bit scary.

Arad shoved his elbow back and into Gunner's ribs. "Back off, quit intimidating my woman, you old buzzard."

Gunner snorted. "You are lucky I like you, wolf boy," the man said but moved back a few steps. "Are you going to allow me the honors?"

Arad reached up and touched her cheek. "Remember what I said earlier, the three different species in you?" Arad asked, and she nodded.

"It would seem the part that is a drinker is rising. Soon, the craving will be so strong you won't be able to control it. The first drink is very important among their kind. Usually, you belong to a family, but you are part of my family." Arad groaned and glanced behind him. "And the old man here has always been part of mine. I don't know how, but he always seems to be there when I need him." Arad turned back to her, lowering Little Tee. "Thea, why don't you take the children in the kitchen and get them a snack."

"Marty, I would like you, Byron, and the doc to be witnesses please," Arad said as everyone cleared out of the room but those Arad had named off.

"Why is this making me nervous?" Catarina leaned over and pulled his head down. "I don't have to sleep with the man, do I?" she whispered.

Arad pulled her into his arms, careful of her shoulder wound. "If I caught you with any other man, that man would be fed to the animals, and you, my dear, would be so sore you wouldn't be able to sit for a damn month. No, Catarina, no one touches your body but me. But, you will be taking your first drink from Gunner, and he will also drink from you, taking you into his family. In other words, no other drinkers will bother you if we come across any."

"Not if they want to live," Gunner said.

Arad snorted. "Gunner's family is one of the oldest, and in his world, he is considered kind of like royalty. It's also one of the reasons why he takes many, many breaks from his family." Arad stepped beside her and turned to face Gunner. "How are your parents?"

"They are well. You know how my father enjoys all the political hub, nub, and Mother with all her charities." Gunner smiled, and Catarina relaxed a little. The man looked less threating.

"Are you ready, Catarina? I will take your blood first, and then, you will take mine. Arad, I'm afraid, after being wounded and such, she might be out for the night when this is over."

"But I always tell Little Tee a story before she goes to bed." She frowned.

"Well then, I'll have to read her one. From the arm." Arad took her hand and lifted it.

"Of course," Gunner said, smiling, taking her

hand. "This will feel uncomfortable at first since you are mate to Arad, but with him close, you should be good," Gunner said to her but looked to Arad who stepped behind her and wrapped his arms around her, nuzzling her neck.

"I'm right here," he whispered as Gunner ran his tongue over her wrist before sinking his fangs into her.

If Arad hadn't been holding on to her, Catarina would have yanked away from him. As it was, she snarled, and at once, Arad nipped at her neck.

"Be nice, all mine, Gunner is doing us a huge honor here," he said, his voice calming her, but when Gunner lifted his gaze, Catarina knew something was wrong.

"Arad?" she said as Gunner calmly stopped feeding and healed the holes in her wrist before stepping back away from her and held up his hand.

"Give me a second, please," Gunner said.

"Why do I get the feeling my so-called father did something again?" Catarina mumbled.

Gunner looked up, and at once, Arad was in front of her. "What?"

She grabbed onto Arad's jeans, stuffing her hands into the back pockets, and rested her head onto his back. Catarina didn't know what it was about his scent, but it seemed to calm her as she rubbed her cheek on his back and closed her eyes.

"I don't know how it's possible, but your woman is family, sister to me," Gunner said.

"What? Okay, Catarina, stop sounding like a damn bird," she grumbled and peaked around Arad.

Both Arad and Gunner stared at her, and she sighed. "I have a little habit of talking to myself out loud, sorry. So, you're not going to rip my head off?" Catarina asked.

* * *

Arad smiled down at his woman. He had a feeling she was going to keep him busy for the rest of their lives. He couldn't help but lean down and place a kiss on her cheek. "What is this about her being a sister?" Arad turned to stare at Gunner.

"I don't know how this happened. The only other sibling I had was my younger brother, and he died over twenty-five years ago," Gunner said. "How old are you Catarina?"

She frowned. "That is kind of rude to ask, but I'm thirty-two, why?"

Gunner shook his head. "Well, that leaves out my brother. It just does not make sense. Oh and Arad..." Gunner held his gaze.

"Shit, your family's coming in, aren't they?" Arad started to pace. "We are scheduled to leave here tomorrow morning. We need to get back and bury our dead." Arad turned and faced his friend.

"Then, you will have another escort, because until we can find out what is going on, Catarina has just gained a brother. Are you ready to feed, little sister?"

"Let's get this over with because a hot bath and my bed are calling my name. Plus, I have three little ones that need to eat and hit the hay if we're getting up early," Catarina mumbled and stepped up next to him. "What do I do?"

Gunner put his wrist up to his mouth and opened up a hole. "Smell, and then, your body will take over knowing what to do."

Arad stayed close to his woman as he watched her eyes glaze over, fangs grew, and she sunk her new fangs into Gunner's wrist, feeding. Arad stepped behind her, seeing Catarina sway as she pulled back.

Her eyes were already closing. "She'll sleep now with the wound and all," Gunner told him. "I'll wait for you."

Arad nodded. "Marty, Byron, see if Thea will feed the kids and get them to put on their PJs; it's time all of them were in bed," he ordered, carrying his woman into her bedroom.

"What can I help you with, Marcus?" Arad asked, laying a sleeping Catarina on the bed and started to strip her of her shoes.

"She's going to be okay?" he asked.

Arad glanced at his grandson. "I promise, Marcus, I'll protect her. No one will hurt Catarina. I'm not my son, you know this."

"What if her father comes after her?" Marcus asked.

"Then, he'll die. Now, go help Thea with the girls, we're all going to be up early. No, we didn't get the man who shot her, but I have a feeling we will see him again," Arad told his grandson before he even could ask. "Off with you. I'll be out in a minute."

The little guy glanced once more at Catarina and spun around, shutting the door behind him.

"He's going to be like his grandfather, I do believe," Catarina said.

He snorted and started to strip her. "We'll see, but I have a feeling we are going to have another Wolf on our hands with that one. Wait 'til you meet Wolf, you'll notice the similarities," he told her, covering her with the blankets.

"I have a nightshirt over there on the chair. I don't sleep in the nude," she mumbled, already closing her eyes.

"You do now, all mine." He placed a kiss on her cheek. "I'll be in after I get everyone settled," he said, getting up, but she hadn't heard him, already out. His woman had a rough day and tomorrow was going to be another one.

Arad closed the door behind him.

Gunner turned to stare at him. "You know something?" he said.

"I don't know if it's my woman, but all the pieces are falling together, and it's not pretty. Let me get the little ones in bed, and I'll explain the story."

Feeding his grandchildren, reading a story to them, and getting them all settled took him longer than he had thought. "Starla, I owe you an apology," he mumbled to his dead wife, now seeing a portion of what his woman had to do each day. He took a beer from his grandson and sat down on the sofa next to Byron.

Gunner sat across from him with what looked like a glass of brandy. "Your woman has a nice bar, I'm quite impressed with her choices. Explain what you think?" Gunner said. "But you have realized what this means, now that she is family."

Gunner smirked. "Seems you are going to get very old, my friend."

Arad snarled at his friend, knowing that he had no choice. He too would have to be a drinker because Arad would be damn if he let his mate go. "Soon, when things settle." He took a sip of his beer and proceeded to inform his friend what he knew.

After about an hour, Arad leaned forward. "Tell me, was your brother's body ever found?" he asked, and Gunner shook his head.

"No, but my parents lost all contact with him, and that only happens when one is gone," Gunner said.

"Maybe not. What if these government guys have a few of you and are studying them? Using them?" Arad asked, earning a snarl from Gunner.

"I think it's time we find this so-called father." Gunner glanced at the door. "If there is some way my brother is alive..." Gunner glanced back at him.

"I'm not using my mate as bait, but if what she tells me is true, if word got out she was going to travel across the border at a certain time, I have a feeling he would be waiting for her," Arad said.

By the time Arad crawled into bed with his woman, it was close to midnight. He reached over and pulled her into his body, holding her tight. Her world had just turned upside down, and Arad would be right there beside her when they found out the truth.

But there was one thing for sure, Arad would make sure that her little girls were found and they would raise them.

Chapter Eight

Catarina took a sip of her coffee, smiling, listening to the waves hit the rocks below. Her hearing had improved, her vision was perfect, and her taste buds were something that was for sure.

It was five o'clock in the morning, and she was wide awake. Arad was snoring away when she had crawled out of the bed, grabbing her clothes. They would be leaving in a few hours, and she was scared out of her mind.

"So, I have your blood, do I?" Catarina asked, knowing Gunner had come up behind her.

He stepped to her side. "Yes, and I'm surprised you are out here alone?"

Catarina shrugged. "I come out here every morning. Watching the sun come up and listening to the waves below seems to settle everything inside me if that makes sense," she said, glancing over her shoulder to see Arad come outside in nothing but jeans.

One thing was for certain, Catarina had lucked out big time when it came to mates because hers was a walking hunk of a man, and god, did he know how to make love.

"Which I would have loved to do again this morning, but I woke to an empty bed," he growled in her head as he came up to her, wrapping his arms around her and nipping her neck.

"Sorry, thought you would need to sleep, plus this is my time out here." She glanced back out at the water.

"Did you contact your folks and inform them what is going on?" Arad asked Gunner, sliding his hands under Catarina's sweater, resting his hands right below her breasts.

"I did, and there will be twenty men at the one crossing we were speaking of last night, and another twenty will meet up with us when we cross at the other point. I'm afraid my mother is insisting on meeting us at your old home. She said no matter if they injected Catarina with our family DNA, you are now family and will be protected as such." Gunner snorted. "As her mate, I'm afraid, that will include you, too." Gunner slapped Arad on the back, jarring her, and she smiled, feeling the snarl behind her.

"You keep slapping me on the back I'm going to bite your ass, and it won't feel good," Arad said. *"What I needed was my woman in my arms when I wake up."*

Catarina snorted and turned seeing the three little ones standing by the back door. "We might as well get an early start," she said and placed a kiss on Arad's cheek.

"Get lost, *brother,*" Arad said. "Take your nieces and nephew inside, have them get dressed, while I show my woman the proper way to say good morning."

Gunner snorted but turned, moving toward the children. "You might also want to inform my little sister about wandering around by herself, especially after someone shot at her last night."

She frowned and looked up at Arad. "There's a proper way to say good morning?"

Arad pulled her into his arms, taking her cup of coffee and dropping it in the grass. "Oh, there are many ways to say good morning, but since you decided to leave our bed, we'll have to make do," Arad said, grabbing a handful of her hair and tilting her head back, staring down at her. "Gunner was right. Until we find out who was taking pot shots, you will not be coming out here alone," he ordered, and before she could say a word of protest, he covered her mouth with his, devouring her.

He tasted of mint and a hint of something else, but Catarina couldn't think as she slid her arms around his neck, holding on, kissing him back. She had been thinking for the past hour since she'd gotten up, wondering why the hell she had accepted Arad so fast into her life and her bed but could find nothing.

All Catarina knew was that his touch was fast becoming an addiction, and she had a feeling his kisses would be, too. He lifted his head and smiled down at her. "That is a little better. I'd still prefer to take you back to bed, but since everyone seems to be up..." He growled and nipped her bottom lip before releasing her hair and setting her back.

"But you will listen to what I said about coming out here in the morning?" he asked, and she sighed.

"Yes, at least until we find the asshole who shot me. Then, we'll see." She looked over her shoulder out at the sea. "I love this view, it's one of the reason's I bought this place." Catarina smiled and looked up at him. "Even when parts of my house were falling apart, it felt as if it was home."

Arad reached down and cupped her cheek. She hadn't realized how tall he was, but standing there next to him, she actually felt dainty, if that was possible with her size-sixteen frame.

He wrapped his arm around her while reaching down and grabbing her cup. "You keep looking at me like that, and we will be going right back in that bedroom; now, behave. We have some packing to do to get everyone ready for this trip."

Arad stopped at the back door and looked down at her. "I need you to promise me you'll do everything I say, all mine. Your life and everyone else's depends on it."

"I should be going myself and meeting you across the border or something. Then, they wouldn't take pot shots at you or the kids," she said, but Arad shook his head.

"Not going to happen, so get that idea out of your head," Arad said, reaching for the door, but Gunner opened it up for them.

"Yes, get that idea out of your head. My parents would be furious, especially since they haven't even gotten to meet you." Gunner gave her look, so she stuck her tongue out at him, the only thing Catarina could think of doing at that minute.

Behind him, Little Tee laughed as did Romy.

"Come on, girls, let's cook up some food. I expect the bears over here soon," Catarina said, moving past Gunner, but he reached out and yanked on her hair.

"Are you a brat, little sister?" he asked, and Arad snorted, following her into the kitchen.

"If I'm not mistaken, you can be a pain in the rear end sometimes, too. And you are very lucky I consider you family, or you would have lost your hand touching what is mine," Arad grumbled.

Catarina ignored them both, pulling out pans, her mind racing with all the things that could go wrong. The thought of one of the children getting hurt had her stopping and taking a deep breath as tears filled her eyes.

Before she knew it, Arad was there wrapping his arm around her. At her legs, Little Tee and Romy were holding onto her, and Marcus had stepped in front of her, wrapping his arms around her.

"We're going to be fine. Your father or whoever is out there is not going to hurt any of us. Take a deep breath, all mine," Arad said as she reached down running her hand over the top of Marcus's head.

"The thought of one of the children getting hurt just takes my breath away." She looked up at Arad. "It's going to be rough going, sorry, but this is so close as to what I went through with my little girls."

"There is no need for you to apologize. I know how much you love our children," Arad said as Byron came up on one side and Marty the other.

"We're not going to let anything happen to our family, and that includes you. Believe me, my grandfather is the best at what he does," Byron said, reaching over and squeezing her shoulder.

Even Marty touched her. She smiled and took a

deep breath. "Well, I guess I just found out the stories were true, you guys are a touchy bunch, aren't ya?" she tried to tease.

Arad grumbled. "I have a reason to touch you and so do the little ones, but there is no reason for you two to be touching all mine," he said.

Catarina couldn't help but laugh as his older grandsons stepped back with smiles on their faces.

"Thank you, all of you." She smiled down at Marcus and winked. "I think I hear our friends. Why don't you get the plates down, and Romy, you can get the silverware. Little Tee, why don't you and your grandfather get the juices out and start pouring some." She leaned down and placed a kiss on each of the kid's head before shooing them off, but Arad wasn't so easy.

He turned her around, his arms tighten around her waist. "All mine?" he questioned.

She looked up and saw the worry. "I guess we're all going to worry 'til this is over. I was thinking you might want to warn Wolf to watch for strangers. If my father knows of you and your family, he'll have others watching them, too."

Arad smiled. "I will inform him, but where Wolf is concerned, he has a little help with the king and queen of the fae. No one can get on our property without Wolf knowing." He kissed her nose. "Lots of bacon... I'm starved."

Catarina laughed. "You got it. You're lucky I just went to the store, and I was expecting the bears."

"I heard that," Thea said, coming over with five more pounds of bacon. "That's why I came prepared, too," her friend said, smiling at her then bumped their hips. "I've got your back, my friend, I've got your back."

* * * *

Arad sat back watching his family and friends eating and laughing. The sheriff and Frita were on their way to pick up Thea's children so they could get on their way. He glanced at his woman and frowned. She had hardly touched her food, and the smile on her face was just a show.

He stood and pulled Catarina's chair out. "If you will excuse us for a few minutes," he told everyone. "Marcus, make sure the kitchen is cleaned up but also make another plate for my mate, she'll be hungry when we are finished."

"What?" Catarina squeaked as he lifted her up and swung her up over his shoulder, placing his hand on her butt as she tried to get down.

"Hold still, Catarina," he ordered, moving through the house to her bedroom, closing the door with his foot before he lowered her to the ground. "You have five minutes to strip out of those clothes before you have more ruined ones," he said, stripping out of his shirt, shoes, and undoing his pants. "Four," he growled, and she jumped, throwing her shirt up over her head, followed by her bra.

"This is insane," she grumbled, but Arad could smell her excitement and see the passion that now replaced the doubt and fear he had seen earlier.

She jumped on one foot trying to get her jeans off, but he didn't wait, reaching over and ripping her panties off with his nails, pushing her face down on the bed. He pulled her hips up and slapped her ass a few times before running his fingers down the crack of her ass to her pussy.

"That is two pairs of panties you owe me, wolf man," she grumbled but pushed her ass back at him as he slid two of his fingers into her.

"I don't think you should wear any, but then again, the last pair had been sexy, we'll see." He thrust his fingers back into her pussy before bringing them up, dripping her juices over ass. "Soon, I'll be making love to you here," he said, sliding two fingers into her slowly. "Have you had anyone make love to you back here, all mine?" he asked, moving his fingers in and out of her, stretching her as he slid his cock into her pussy, earning a moan.

"No," Catarina whispered into the bed as she grabbed onto the blankets as he slowly made love to her all the while keeping his fingers inside her ass.

"I think we need to pick up a few plugs for you, too, along with that paddle," he told her before removing his fingers and covering her body with his.

She looked back and smiled. "Am I mated to a dirty old man?" she teased.

"Old, I'll show you old, and honey, it's not dirty to add some spice to our love life. I personally can't wait to see you tied and open for me to do whatever I want. Hishi Karada is one of the most beautiful things I've seen, and I can't wait to experiment with you, all mine, but that will wait until I can take my time." He placed a kiss on the side of her neck, reaching under her, one hand going to her breast and the other to her clit.

"Now, let's see if I can make you scream so everyone can hear you down the street, shall we?" he said before letting go, thrusting into her hard and quick, hitting that spot inside her at the same time he worked her little nub.

It didn't take long before he felt her body start to shake and her pussy tighten on his cock. He hated that all he had given her were quick, hard lovings, but soon, he would worship his warrior woman. Arad smiled at the term, biting down on her shoulder, sending her over the edge.

He had been right, her scream of passion would be heard as she came unglued in his arms, but Catarina wasn't the only one who the others would hear as he released her shoulder, letting go a howl, making sure everyone knew she was his, claiming her again.

"When I get the energy, I'm so going to clobber you. What the hell was that howl?" She glanced over at him as he fell to the side of her, slipping out of her but pulling her to him, holding on to her.

"Of course, I had to inform everyone you were mine and only mine. No man, well any sane man, will come close to you now," he told her, nipping her nose.

She rested her head on his chest, quiet for a couple of seconds. "Arad, I really am scared. I don't think that vampire lady should have sent me that book. I'm not a warrior," she said, looking up at him. "I just survive."

He rolled her over, placing her under him again. "You are a true warrior, my mate. What you went through with those that were supposed to be your family, not to mention that excuse of a man who took your babies. Let's not forget the struggle you have each day to stay sober. No, you are a warrior, all mine, my warrior. The children's warrior." He gave her a quick kiss and jumped up. "Get dressed, the sheriff is here. We need to get going, but you will eat as we drive toward the border. I want you at full strength, understood?" he told her as he grabbed his pants, sliding them on.

"No underwear?" she questioned, and he smiled, shaking his head.

"Nope, never have, and I have a feeling that is a good thing," he said, handing her jeans to her. "No underwear, all mine, we might need to shift fast, and it hinders you," Arad said, dressing quickly, hearing the bikes coming down the street.

She didn't say a word, dressing quickly and moving to the door, but he pulled her back into his arms. "Deep breath, all mine. I will not have you hyperventilating."

Catarina threw up her hands and turned, glaring at him. "See, I'm not a damn warrior! I'm a damn chicken shit because the thought of crossing that border is terrifying me, Arad," she said, the last part coming out in a whisper, and a single teardrop rolled down her cheek.

He reached up and cupped her cheek. "The Fates wouldn't have given me you if they didn't think you were a true warrior. You have been through hell and back but survived, and we will survive this together. You will not be alone again, all mine."

When they both stepped into the living room, Arad was glad he had a hold of his woman as her body shook. The sheriff held a man in the room, cuffed, and the glare he was giving his woman had Arad snarling.

The man's gaze jumped to Arad, and he stepped back.

"Who is this?"

"Two of my deputies caught him running in the woods; he has the same weapon that shot at your woman. His name is—" The sheriff started to say.

"Andrew Batcher, my ex-husband," Catarina said, finding her voice and legs. "Where are my girls," she snarled.

"I gave them to your father. You gave birth to two freaks. Let your father have them, but what you put me through... Did you know our daughters shifted right there in the middle of the street? They attacked a boy. I was kicked out of the town, all because of you. You should be dead!" he snarled and tried to lunge at her.

"You gave my babies to my father," she screamed and lunged herself, snarling, half shifting, but Arad held onto her.

"Get him out of here. Find out what you can from him and call me. I want those two little girls found," Arad ordered, lifting his mate up and carrying her outside to the ocean view she liked so much, needing her calm before they left.

His heart broke, hearing her sobs as she buried her face against his chest, holding onto his shirt. "I should have been with them. He has my babies."

"If they are like their mother, they will survive 'til we can get to them. I promise, no matter what, we will get them back." Arad snarled, holding onto her, hating like hell that he could do nothing right then and there.

Chapter Nine

C atarina knew Andrew would be killed eventually, and right now, she didn't give a damn, she was so furious with herself and him. She glared over at Arad as he made her eat the plate of food and the fact he hadn't allowed her to go after the creep who had taken her little girls from her. All she had wanted to do was rip his face off, but for the first time, Arad had taken her into the bedroom and given her a true spanking, promising her that the sheriff had better ways to get information out of her ex, but she still resented her sore ass.

Catarina flinched when she reached down to get her drink and heard the three little ones in the back seat giggling, watching them.

She peeked over her shoulder and winked at Little Tee. "You're lucky you are driving," she grumbled. "It still hurts."

"You do know all these sass remarks are adding up, and it was meant to hurt. *All spankings are not for pleasure, all mine.*" Arad glanced at her, and the look he gave her had her toes curling.

"I'm sick that is all there is to it." She shook her head and stabbed a sausage, stuffing it into her mouth. *Who the hell gets excited at the thought of a man paddling her butt, sick.* She stared out at the landscape as Arad squeezed her leg.

"*Not sick, just some people need the little extra,*

there is nothing wrong with it. I happen to enjoy seeing your round butt pink from my hand," he told her.

"You still should have let me rip his face off. He could still speak," she grumbled.

Arad laughed. "You are a vicious one, that is for sure, but not to worry, he will get what is coming to him. Finish eating, all mine, we only have another hour of driving before we meet Wolf's team. We'll stop for about an hour. I want all of you to stick together, is that understood?" Arad glanced in the rearview mirror, looking at the children. "I'm counting on you, Marcus, to help me today. I need you to make sure no one comes near the women."

Catarina frowned. *"Don't you think that is a little much to put on the little guy?"* she asked.

"No, he still is in protective mode. Going back has already put him on alert. Look back at him, you'll see the wolf very close to the surface. Your wolf should be able to recognize this, also. Always trust your wolf's instincts. Our animals can sense things way before our human side can, which will give us the advantage when it comes to fighting them, but it won't protect us from their darts." Arad snarled the last part, and she knew he was thinking of his son.

Without thinking of it, Catarina reached out and took his hand into hers. "I'm sorry. I wish I could have helped more," she told him, forgetting everything about their little grumble. "I guess my father and his bunch of goons have affected us all in some way. It just sucks it wasn't in a positive way." Catarina's stomach tightened. "I have a feeling these idiots aren't finished either. I was thinking about this theory that I was abducted from a couple as a child." She looked up at him.

"You know someone had to have helped him. There is no way a human could have gotten by a wolf, bear, or whatever this child was. So, he has people here that can help him. I bet that is how Andrew found me. The question is why they left me alone for so long?"

"If that is the case, most likely, they were waiting to see if you shift or something would happen, but you do have a point." Arad pulled away from her and grabbed his phone.

Catarina listened as Arad explained to Ronnie what she believed, informing him to tell no one about her whereabouts and to have everyone be on alert for possible threats. As she listened to Arad speak, the authority in his voice spoke volumes.

This man, her mate, if what she believed were true, was one very powerful man. She smiled. Arad even made her SUV look small as he sat behind the steering wheel. His grayish black hair, in a braid down his back, and how could she forget his eyes. Once he turned his full attention on her, it was as if she were his world, which was weird in itself. No one had ever put her first.

His hand slid under her ass, and Arad squeezed, causing her to jump and glare at him. "What was that for? That hurt!" she slapped his arm, earning gasps from the back seat, which had her sighing.

"Listen, you three. You have to remember I was raised as a human. I'm going to do things that might not be right for your kind. Well, our kind, so when I lightly slap your grandfather on the arm, it's like a natural reflex with me." She looked at Arad. "Especially where I spent a few of my years."

Arad smiled and cupped her cheek. "Then, it is a good thing I remind you often of what you are and who you are with."

"Down," Catarina yelled, yanking Arad down, seeing the car pull up on the driver's side with two men with guns pointed at their car.

Two shots shattered their windows as Arad stepped onto the gas, speeding ahead of the car. "Who's hurt?" he snarled as she heard the crash before jumping up and looking in the back seat.

Sure enough, Marcus had used his body to shield the two little ones. Catarina could see pieces of glass on his back and all over the floor. "Marcus!" she yelled and was about to climb into the back seat when Arad pulled over to the side of the road.

"Talk to me, Marcus." Arad got out of the car, scanning around before opening the back door as Marcus lifted his head up, his wolf's eyes met hers.

"Shit, Arad, his head," Catarina snarled and looked at both girls, who appeared to be fine but scared.

"I've got him," Arad said as their car was surrounded by Arad's men and other men she had no idea who they were.

"Arad?" she questioned, climbing into the back to be with the girls, and talk about a pain in the ass when you have a full-figured woman climbing over the seat. "So, going to lose weight," she mumbled.

"You will not, and they are all our men, which I would like to know how the hell that car got so close to us?" He snarled the last part. "Bryon, we need a new car."

"Got one already coming," Gunner said, peeking into the back seat, looking her over then the two little ones who were now clinging to her when she unstrapped them from their seats.

"Watch the glass, little sister. You do know you saved your alpha?" Gunner said.

"How could you know," she grumbled. "And I'd do that for anyone," she grumbled and carefully climbed out of the car with the two little ones attached to her. She looked behind her, seeing the car that had taken pot shots at them and snarled.

"Easy there, all mine, we have them," Arad said, rubbing her back and placing a kiss on her cheek. "The new car is here. We have twenty minutes to go 'til we reach Wolf's men, but I want to know how these idiots knew which way we were going? Are we walking right into a trap or what?" Arad said and guided them to a large black beast.

"Okay, who has the nuts," she asked, looking around. "I smell nuts," Catarina stated as Arad stopped and sniffed the air.

"Let's use Gunner's car, shall we? Gunner, you are driving, and you might want to find out who the hell sent that car," Arad snarled at him.

"Why?" Gunner said, glancing toward the car then at them as they moved past the offending vehicle, which was upside down. Marty and Byron followed them close as they walked down the road.

"Because if I'm not mistaken, there is a bomb

attached to that car."

Catarina hugged Little Tee and squeezed Romy's hand as she looked up at Arad. "They really want me dead, don't they?"

* * *

Arad helped settle his mate and the children in Gunner's car, all the while her words had his wolf wanting to take off and hunt down each and everyone that sought her. He shut the door and turned. "We are not moving from here 'til we know what is going on. Someone knows where we are, and I will not risk my family again."

"Call Wolf, see if his in-laws could help out here. We can't sit out here in the open. Hell, maybe they could take the women and children back to Wolf's while we deal with this threat," Marty snarled.

Arad glanced back at the car while pulling out his phone.

On the first ring, Wolf answered. *"What's wrong?"* he asked.

"They know where we are," Arad said as said car that they were supposed to take exploded. "And that was the backup car you just heard," Arad snarled.

Before he could say another word, Wolf was there with two blond, tall men. Wolf scanned the area then down at the car behind him where Thea was now sitting in the car speaking with Catarina and the children.

"Let us take the children, you can..." Wolf got out, but Arad snarled, stopping the rest of his words.

"She has been shot at, and now, a bomb was placed under that car for her. I want my mate safe, not as a damn walking target." He ran his hand over his head. "Plus, the children will not go anywhere without her."

His mate's shout from the car had him turning as she pushed open the door and hopped out next to him. "Where the hell are they?" she snarled. "Do you know how upset Little Tee is going to be. She just started to talk!" Catarina yelled as Arad pulled her into his arms, trying to calm her.

Thea stepped out of the car, moving in next to Catarina.

"They are safe. Wolf had them sent right to the house where you and Thea are going now." Arad looked up at Wolf, who nodded.

Before he could kiss her goodbye, she and Thea were gone, along with the two men. "They will be safe, but you better be, too, and find out who the hell is leaking information," Wolf ordered, and Arad snorted, his grandson so much like him.

A small smile appeared on Wolf's lips. "And don't get hurt, old man. I know your reflexes are a little slow now." Wolf disappeared before Arad could lunge at him.

"I'll show you how slow," he grumbled. "Byron, unhook my bike." He looked at his friend Gunner. "You ready for a ride?"

Gunner smiled. "Just like old times. Glad I didn't feed this morning."

In less than ten minutes, he and Gunner were on his bike and ready to go. "I want the rest of you to come up like nothing has happened. We'll find out who has double-crossed us and wait for you." He looked to Marty and Byron. "Both of you better be there, understood?"

Byron smiled all cocky as Marty shook his head. "Worry about yourself, old man," Marty said.

"Don't get cocky, Marty. Never underestimate your enemy. Anyone around us right now could be a traitor, remember that," Arad said before taking off, leaving them to do as he instructed.

"You know who betrayed us?" Gunner asked.

"As for the ones we are about to meet, yes, but there is also one we left back there with my grandsons," Arad informed his friend.

"And you left him there alive?" Gunner asked, shocked.

"Yes, because as soon as we left, this person will reveal themselves. Marty already knows who it is but is waiting. Byron, he's still got more training, and seeing his brother in action might help wake him up," Arad explained.

"I think we still should have destroyed the man."

"No, we wouldn't have found the second one then," Arad said as he listened to Marty explain what happened thirty minutes later.

"Let me guess, Marty was cussing you out." Gunner laughed, and he couldn't help but also laugh, even though he was also very proud of Byron, finding the second one before Marty and stopping them from alerting the others that they were coming.

"They are just like their grandfather," Gunner

said.

"I won't argue," Arad said. "It's a waste of time."

"I won't argue," Arad said. "It's a waste of time."

Chapter Ten

Catarina was so going to kill a wolf, she thought as all three of the children had run to her and Thea as soon as they appeared in some huge log cabin, which could have been in one of those million-dollar-homes magazines.

Catarina took a deep breath and glared at the children's oldest brother. "Marcus, please stop growling at your brother." She put Romy on the couch with Little Tee next to her.

"He could be like my father, and Granddad isn't here to protect you. He told me to protect all of you," he said, puffing up his little chest, moving to stand in front of them.

"That he did, but I do believe he said that for the other men, you know, the ones that were shooting at us, and I must say, I'm so proud of you." Catarina placed her hand on his shoulder. "You stopped the glass from getting on your sisters, but you have a few spots I need to take a look at, and I can't do that if you're standing there growling at him." She glared at the man who stood there, not saying a word, watching.

"You know it would help if you backed up a bit and quit staring at him," Catarina said as Thea nudged her.

"Um, he's an alpha," she whispered in Catarina's ear.

"And? I have three children here who are scared out of their damn minds, let alone traumatized from my asshole father and his goons, not to mention the fact the children do not feel safe here," she snarled.

"Oh, for Pete sakes, Wolf, back up and give your brother and sisters some space. It's obvious your brother is not going to back down 'til you do, and he is bleeding," a woman said, pushing Wolf out of the way and stepping around him, but the man named Wolf pulled her back to his side.

"What did I tell you about placing yourself in front of me?" He reached down and squeezed her ass, making her jump, reminding Catarina of what Arad had done earlier.

She snorted. "See, Marcus, your brother is just like your grandfather, a pain in the butt, literally."

For the first time, Catarina saw a smile on Wolf, and Marcus took a deep breath, glancing back at her, smiling.

"I really am okay," he said.

"That is good, but the glass still needs to come out, Marcus. You don't want to heal and have your skin grow over the glass. Now, come here so I can clean you up a little. By the way, I'm Catarina Wahlberg, and the one that is ready to pass out is Thea. Thea, sit down. Could I get a washcloth and trash can maybe so I can clean Marcus up?" she asked and stopped. "Well, crap, we don't have any clothes or anything to change into." She frowned.

"I'm Tobie, Wolf's mate, and welcome. No one here is going to hurt you, Marcus. Wolf wasn't infected with the darts, and he can't be," the woman said and turned to look at Wolf. "You going to release me so I can get what she needs?"

"Fine, but you're getting awful snippy." He frowned down at her. Wolf released her and moved to sit across from them. "My brother and sisters have formed a bond with you? I'm sorry if I'm standoffish, as my mate would say, but after what we have been through, what they have been through, I will not risk their lives even if my little brother objects." Wolf sat back and smiled. "I have to say, my grandfather moves fast for an old man."

"Wolf!" Tobie yelled at him, coming into the room, but she said nothing to the rude asshole, not sure if she liked him or not.

Ignoring his remark, Catarina thanked Tobie for the washcloth and proceeded to clean Marcus up, pulling bits of glass out of his back.

It wasn't as if Catarina didn't already think they had moved too fast, but damn, one look and she was a big glob of Jell-O.

"I so love Jell-O and will personally lick and suck every inch of you as soon as I show my grandson what manners are," Arad said.

"He only speaks the truth, we did move awful fast. I didn't even get a date out of you. How easy does that make me?" she asked, wiping down Marcus's back.

"We will have plenty of dates, I promise, to court you when things settle down," Arad said, quickly disconnecting their link.

Wolf leaned forward. "You were speaking with my grandfather?" Wolf flinched, but a smile broke out. "I owe you an apology. Seems my grandfather is not too happy with me right now." Wolf cracked his knuckles. "It's been ages since me and the old man faced each other; it should be interesting, to say the least."

Catarina smiled and patted Marcus's back. "You're good, Marcus, and again, I'm proud of you covering your sisters and so is your grandfather," Catarina said, earning a quick glance back at her and a nod before sitting down at her feet.

Wolf smiled. "I would like to personally thank you for taking in my little sisters and brother. All of us were worried sick when we found out how far my father had gone."

"I'm afraid even my grandfather couldn't reverse the damage done by the drug that was released here on Earth," Tobie said, sitting on the arm of Wolf's chair, as another came into the room.

Once more, Marcus snarled and scooted back, leaning against her legs. "Calm, Marcus. Remember what your grandfather told you." Catarina reached down and squeezed his shoulder.

"Catarina, these are my adopted parents. They live here with us until their place is finished. Alvin and Patricia Droan," Tobie introduce the couple.

The man tilted his head to the side, kneeling before Marcus. "You are alpha and very protective of her. It is a pleasure to meet you, little man." Alvin held out his hand to Marcus.

At first, Catarina didn't think Marcus would take the man's hand, but eventually, he did, shaking it. "Marcus and thank you. She's our mother now, our family."

"Our mother is being prepared to be buried, Marcus. Catarina is a nice woman who helped you but not our mother." Wolf stood. "Excuse me. I have work to do and make sure everything is set for the ritual." Wolf moved toward the front door, at least that is what she believed it was but stopped and glanced at her.

"I still think it best that my sisters and brother stay here with us. Plus, you and grandfather need time together." With those parting words before Marcus or anyone could say anything, Wolf was out the door, slamming it shut behind him.

"Well, that went well, didn't it?" Tobie said, frowning at the door where her mate used to be. "I'm sorry, Catarina, this has been so hard on Wolf. The two people he was closet to were his mom and his grandfather."

Catarina flinched. "And I seem to be taking both of their places, which I really don't mean to." She rubbed her chin on Little Tee's head. "I just couldn't see the three of them separated, and I had a big house. Plus, I guess, I needed the children as much as they needed me."

"Bad man took her twins. Now, she has us," Romy said and lifted her chin up, and Catarina laughed.

"Be nice, Romy. Tobie is your sister now by marriage, family," Catarina said.

"You're our family, and I'm not staying here. I want to go back home." Romy curled up tighter at her side.

Catarina looked up at Thea, who shook her head.

"I had a feeling this would happen. It happened with my boys, and I see it a little now that Marty has informed them about being my mate. It's going to take us all time to work things out," Thea said and ran her hand over Romy's head.

Tobie stood. "Mom, would you show Catarina where we set up the master room. Catarina, there is another bedroom attached to it, which we set up a few beds for the children right now. Thea, there is a room across the hall from hers that you are welcome to have." Tobie moved to the door. "Oh, and my grandmother has placed clothes for all of you in the room, knowing you didn't have anything. If you will excuse me, I'm going to find my mate and make sure he's okay, and yes, Dad, I know, guards." Tobie rolled her eyes, and Catarina couldn't but help smile.

"Tobie, please tell Wolf I really didn't mean to take anyone's place. But the children mean the world to me, too," Catarina said, placing Little Tee in Thea's arms before she stood, moving to and hugging Tobie. "We'll all figure out something. Again, thank your family," she said.

"There is no reason to apologize. You have done nothing wrong. We are on our way there. The traitors have been taken care of, and we actually caught two of your father's men, but he wasn't here. I'm sorry, all mine," Arad told her, and she closed her eyes.

"He'll follow you. See if the men have trackers on them. I found two on me before I settled where I am. He buries them under the skin, and please, be careful." Catarina turned and held out her

hand.

"Come, let's get cleaned up. Your grandfather will be here in an hour, and then, we'll get things settled," she said as Romy came over, taking her hand. Marcus moved in front of them as always, while Thea carried Little Tee, her family no matter what anyone said.

* * *

Arad was fuming. Not only were the children upset, but also Wolf had insulted his woman twice.

"You need to calm down, my friend. The children and your woman do not need to see you so angry. Plus, if what you told me of your grandson, you know he's having a hard time with the passing of his mother," Gunner said.

Both men were dirty from the fight at the border. He glanced back where he had left his friend. It would seem Arad wasn't the only one who had found his mate. He snorted, remembering seeing the book in Isabella's little cubby where she worked, but it was too bad she had suffered a killing bullet.

"Don't worry about me, how is your woman doing? I still can't believe you found her, talk about rotten timing though," Arad tried to calm down talking to his friend.

"She will make it. We are traveling toward you, but at a slower rate since I don't want to jar the wound open that is just now starting to close. When Isabella wakens, she will be one of ours and my mate," Gunner sighed.

"You had no choice, she would have died. It seems we both will be doing a lot of courting in the next few weeks." Arad said, going over everything that had happened at the crossing.

They had been waiting for Gunner and Arad to pull up, but what they weren't expecting was the fact his friend could also shift into any animal he wished. No one was expecting the rat that scoped out the area and took care of two of the men before he even got to approach.

But neither of them had seen the female come out of the building to see what was going on as gunfire started to erupt. Not even Gunner was fast enough to stop the bullet that entered her heart as she stepped in front of one of those that had been waiting for them.

They were lucky, the Canadian authorities had seen the attack and the deaths of two of their officers. The one man had been shot in the head, and there had been no saving him, but Arad had explained that Gunner was going to heal the second, his mate, but she would have to stay with him until the healing could take place.

After reassuring the officials that they would have this woman call when she able to, Arad had hopped onto his bike as the rest of their group pulled up before he had gotten some information about Catarina's father and the locations he could be at. He would send out a team as soon as he got home to search for his woman's daughters, and god help the man if he harmed them at all.

Twenty minutes later, he was pulling down the road toward his cabin when he spotted his grandson leaning against the railing, waiting. He pulled his bike off to the side of the road and shut it off. It would seem Arad wouldn't have to hunt down his grandson after all.

He took off his jacket and gloves, placing them on the bike as he rose to get off the bike. "I appreciate the fact you came to me, that I didn't have to hunt you down," he said, and Wolf snorted.

"Don't want you to use up too much energy because I'm going to cream you, old man. Oh, and by the way, the children will be staying here with us," Wolf snarled. "I don't want my sisters and brother with anyone connected to that asshole."

"You do realize that you are only adding to the fire?" Arad said, stalking toward his grandson. "And the children will be going back. I promised them, and I keep my promises. They will live with me and my mate, who you have insulted, hurt a few times tonight. I taught you better," he snarled and attacked when Wolf turned to the right.

His grandson was about to learn a few more lessons by the time he was done with him tonight. In two movies, Arad had his grandson down face first. "For someone who talks so much..."

Before Arad could get the words out, Wolf had him on his back, smiling down at him. "Had to give you a little leeway, after all, you just got finished battling, didn't want you to feel useless, old man." Wolf smiled, and Arad couldn't help but smile back but also managed to get away and jumped up.

Wolf slowly got up and glanced behind Arad.

"Thought I would let you know Catarina and the children are being shown to your side of the cabin.

My grandmother has provided clothes for them since all of their belongings were destroyed." Tobie stepped around.

"Thank you, Tobie, and not all of their belongings. The children and Catarina only packed enough for a visit here. We will be going back as soon as the services are finished." His gaze didn't leave Wolf's. "Do not interfere here, Wolf. I taught you to hold off judgment on someone, to get to know them. Why has Catarina fluffed up your fur?"

"She will draw that bastard. I don't want my sisters and brother around that," Wolf snarled, pulling Tobie to his side.

"Not if he is taken out before we leave, but the children will not stay here, Wolf. It reminds them too much of their father, and right now, they can't handle it." Arad took a deep breath. "Something happened to them, especially to Little Tee, before your father killed your mother, and right now, the only reason she is hanging on is Catarina. No, Wolf, on this, you are wrong. The children stay with Catarina. We will be here at least a week, get to know my mate before you judge her," Arad said, moving to his bike. "Plus, you know she isn't human. If all the reports are right, she too was taken as a child. Not to mention that bastard who calls himself her family now has her two little girls, and I'm not going to allow that prick to hurt those little ones any more than he has."

Tobie kissed Wolf's cheek. "Your grandfather is right. Give her a chance. Those little ones are not going to leave her, Wolf. They love her, and even I can see how much they need her. Help your grand-father get her babies and destroy that man who has hurt so many. Arad, I will help Catarina in any way I can; after all, she is family now."

Arad threw his leg over his bike. "Thank you, Tobie. I will discuss later what we found out, but my friend Gunner is about twenty minutes behind us with a woman who was fatally shot. Seems my old friend found his mate." He shook his head. "That vampire friend of mine sure does get around. This woman even had a book in her work-station. Oh, and Wolf, you insult what is mine again, grandson or not, I'll knock you on your ass. There is no reason to be rude or nasty." Without another word, Arad put on his coat and gloves be-fore starting the bike and taking off. The need to see his woman and the children were strong. Yes, they were a family, and he'd be damn if his grand-son were going to tear apart what had already started to form—their family unit.

Chapter Eleven

C atarina lifted her head and smiled. Arad was close. She took a deep breath and looked around at the small family room in this side of the wing. All three little ones had taken showers and were relaxing, watching TV while she gathered her things to take one next.

Thea came into the room. "I'm all done, your turn. I'll watch the kids." Her friend smiled, shooing her hands at her.

Catarina grabbed the jeans and sweater she had found, making her way into the master suite. One thing was for sure, Arad's master suite was huge, but she did feel a little out of place, wondering if his first wife had been there, sharing the room.

Stripping out of her dirty clothes, Catarina started to go over the last two days and shook her head. One thing was for sure, this being a shifter was so different. Would she ever learn their ways? The fact that Catarina could even now feel Arad getting closer had her body revving up, which was weird in itself. Never had she had these feelings for a man, let alone crave his touch, but there was no stopping her body's reaction.

She stepped into the warm shower just as Catarina heard the bathroom door open and close. After a few minutes without a sound, she turned to see Arad leaning against the counter, naked,

108

watching her.

He gripped his cock, stroking it. "Why would you want to stop what you are feeling? Do I make you uncomfortable, all mine?"

"Not at all. It's the whole situation, Arad. In two days, I'm mated, can't get enough of you, and back in the US when I said I'd never come here again. Then, there is the fact my so-called father might not be my father but a man who experimented on me. Oh, let's not forget my crazy ex who handed over my babies..." she cried, tears rolled down her cheeks as Arad stepped into the shower and pulled her into his arms.

"Shh, I've got you, all mine. Cry, little wolf, cry, let it out," he said, kissing the top of her head, holding her. His arms felt like a safety net, that once he wrapped them around her, she was safe.

She snorted and looked up at him. "I really think that vampire psychic lady needs help," Catarina said and reached up to wipe her tears. "Warrior woman my ass," she mumbled and rested her head on Arad's chest.

His growl should have warned her, but he was quick as one of his big hands came down on her wet ass, and talk about hurting.

She tried to jump away, but he held her in place.

"Never, and I mean never, let me hear you degrade yourself again, Catarina. If it is one thing I won't put up with, it is that." He swatted her again before reaching up and grabbing hold of her chin.

Catarina tried to pull away from him, even to the point of kicking his leg, but all she did was hurt her own damn foot and almost fell in the shower.

"Let me go," she snarled and glared up at him, the big jerk.

"No, you will hear me on this, all mine. Do you really believe the Fates would put you with a man who is…" he paused for a minute, thinking.

"Bossy, a pain in my sore ass," she grumbled.

He smiled. "I was going to say dominant, alpha, but I like that I'm a *pain in your ass* part." He leaned down and nipped her nose. "Who wouldn't stand up for three little children, even after her heart was broken from having her own taken from her. Who else would share her past, knowing that some might think ill of her but not caring? A warrior, one who has a heart as big as that ocean your home sits on. You, Catarina, are my warrior woman, and together, we will grow. If I'm not mistaken, my grandson told me there were exercises for us to work on. We'll do that as soon as we are settled." He lifted her up and placed her up against the shower wall, staring down at her.

"Wrap your legs around me, all mine." He waited as he squeezed her butt cheeks, which had her jumping and glaring at him.

"That hurts," she said but doing as he demanded.

"Quit complaining, you and I both know you like a little pain." He released one of her butt cheeks, sliding his hand between them. "As I suspected." He thrust two of his fingers into her, holding them there. "All mine, before we head back home here in Canada, we will have your girls, that is a promise."

"How can you promise that when we don't even

know where he is. Even you aren't a miracle worker." She smiled, wrapping her arms around him. "But I thank you for trying."

Arad leaned down and nipped her bottom lip, and she snorted. "You like to bite a lot."

"Umm, I will be nipping, sucking, and marking your body, but trust me, all mine. I have extra help coming in to help us find your babies."

Her heart jumped. Did she hope?

When Catarina met his gaze, she could almost see his certainty. "Then, let us both hope he does not hurt them and that we get there in time."

"Think positive, all mine." Once more, Arad pulled his fingers out of her and replaced them with his cock, thrusting into her. "But now, you will concentrate on us."

She gripped his shoulders and knew once more that they were digging into his shoulders as his pace picked up. "That is all I do lately is think of you..." she moaned the last part.

* * *

Arad smiled, burying himself inside his woman. Little did she know, already Arad had men coming in to help with the hunt for her children. Not to mention the fact that Gunner and his family would pull no stops to help them since she was now considered a part of their intimate family.

When he had pulled up to the house, Arad had known his woman was bordering on screaming or crying. It broke his heart, watching her in the shower, her mind going through everything that had happened over the last two days.

Yes, their life, their world was much different from that of the humans. She and Gunner's mate would learn fast what it meant to be the mate of two of the most powerful men in their world.

But yet, he had a feeling his woman would also show him how to live again, to love and believe in the impossible.

He jerked back and glared down at his woman, who had just bitten him in the shoulder.

"You're lacking here, get your mind back in the play," she snarled at him, but Arad could see the smile in her eyes.

"I apologize, all mine," he said, lifting her legs up, placing them onto his shoulders, giving him better penetration, thrusting in and out of her.

He smiled when he swore her eyes rolled back and she tried to hold onto him but couldn't keep her grip as he gave her all his attention. If it was one thing, Arad was not one to let any distraction get in his way of what he wanted, and right them, he wanted his mate squeezing the hell out of his cock and his seed pouring into her.

Her head snapped up. "A child? Are you sure?" she squeaked as he thrust into her again.

"Yes, a child, our child," he said. "Reach down and play with your button, all mine."

At first, she hesitated, but soon, Catarina slid her hand down between them, playing with herself.

"That's it, faster, harder," he growled, watching, feeling her pussy squeeze his cock, one more thing to send her over.

He let go of her ass cheek but returned to it, spanking her already sore ass. Her eyes got big, and her body started to shake, but she wasn't the only one who was flying as Arad released his seed into her. Her body milking his.

"We are pulling onto the road," Gunner informed him.

"Pull right up to the house. I have a spare room for you and your mate," Arad said, lowering Catarina's legs down, getting a moan from her.

When she could stand, he cupped her cheeks, looking down at her. "I'm really sorry my grandson hurt you, but he has been warned; it won't happen again." He kissed her lips softly. "You are so beautiful inside and out. The rest of our party is arriving. Come, we have plans to make, and we're going to need your help with Gunner's mate," he said, reaching and quickly washing them both down before turning the water off.

She frowned as he handed her a towel. "What do you mean you need my help? What is wrong with his mate?" she asked, watching.

Arad met her gaze. "She used to be a human but was shot when the ambush happened. Gunner had no choice but to bring her into our world to save her."

"She doesn't know what happened yet, does she?"

"No, right now, her body is healing. Gunner is pulling up with her in the van. I'll put them in the room across from where Thea is," Arad said, watching as she pulled on a pair of jeans.

The jeans hugged her ass, and all he wanted to

do was rip the pants right off her.

She laughed, opening the door. "Tonight, wild man, tonight. We have work to do and children to reassure, especially coming from you." Her voice dropped down. "All of them are worried. They know Wolf wants them to stay here. Little Tee isn't eating much. I'm worried about her." She looked out the door toward the little family room he had in his wing.

Arad stepped behind her and wrapped his arms around her from behind. "I'll be right out, and they're coming home with us. Even I can tell this is not a place to raise those three. They need a fresh break. As I did. You are that wind, bringing us together as a family and giving us all hope." He kissed the side of her neck and smacked her ass. "Go on; I'll be right out."

She glared at him but placed a kiss on his chin. "You're lucky I like you, wild man," Catarina grumbled.

"Like?" he asked, cupping her cheek.

Catarina patted his chest. "I'm getting there, Arad, but the last time I gave those words to a man, gave him ten years of my life, and two beautiful girls…" She looked away from him.

"All mine, I promise, I'm not going anywhere, and if it takes days, months, or even a year, I'll wait for those words because you show us in many ways how much you care."

"Go on, seems Wolf is waiting for us now." Arad stepped into the bedroom, going to his dresser, grabbing a fresh shirt and pants, dressing quickly, not yet trusting his grandson with his mate.

"*His mate is with him, along with two males and another female. Please do not allow this between us to interfere with your family,*" she said, and he could feel her discomfort.

Two minutes later, he stepped out into the family room, going right to his woman, taking Little Tee from her arms before sitting down next to Catarina. "How can we help you, Wolf?" He nodded to Tobie and her family behind her. "My friend Gunner and his mate should be pulling up to the house any minute. We need to get her settled before we speak."

Wolf nodded to him, but his grandson's gaze went to Catarina. "We might have a way to find Catarina's children and have them here by tonight," Wolf said.

Chapter Twelve

The thought of having her children there had her jumping up, regardless of the look Wolf was giving her. "What do I have to do?"

"Wolf, watch where you step." Arad stood up next to her, wrapping his arm around her, caging her to his side.

Wolf laughed. "So little faith in me, but I guess I can understand why." Wolf sighed and stepped forward, bowing his head to Catarina. "I would like to apologize for what happened earlier again. You are family, and I accept this." He glanced at Little Tee and reached up to touch her cheek, and she snarled, burying her face into Arad's neck.

"I'm sorry, but when I first got the three of them, none of them said a word, but Little Tee, she's still battling her demons as I'm afraid my two little ones will be, too." Catarina reached over and rubbed her hand on the child's head. "Maybe, if you do find my babies, we can all heal as a family, because I have a feeling that prick also harmed my girls."

Arad frowned and glanced down at her. "Why? What haven't you told me?" he asked, and she snorted.

"I don't know how to explain it." She placed her hand on her heart. "It's in here. For a while, I felt as if something was wrong, but who knows, maybe it's just me being silly." Catarina shrugged when the woman behind Tobie stepped forward.

"My name is Mary MacGoraidh, I'm Tobie's grandmother. You are feeling the bond of the mother. Believe me, I know. I knew when my daughter died, but I wanted to deny it. Trust your instincts." She looked back at her husband, and he nodded. "My father is the one that has offered to help you find your babies. I wish we could have done this for my daughter, but she knew how to block us. Your babies won't." Mary glanced at Catarina. "My father will have to go inside you, in your head. There is a connection you have with your babies, this is the connection my father will use to find your babies if you allow us to help you."

Arad stiffened next to her. "If you do this, how would we get the children out?"

The man bowed, the true king of the fae, Ridge Leafray. "I do not need any help getting the children out, but having your men there to take care of the others that most likely he has there experimenting on would be helpful."

Arad nodded. "Gunner is here with his mate. I have to show him to his room, but Gunner should be here. There is a chance his brother is being held there."

"Go, we can wait a few minutes." Catarina reached over, taking Little Tee out of his arms, the little girl whined but realized who had her and settled in her arms. "I've got you, little one. Soon, you'll have two more girls to play with," Catarina said, sitting back down, waving Arad off.

"I'll allow him to read my mind while you are

gone, then we'll go from there. Go, nothing will happen to me," Catarina said, hoping it was true.

Arad snarled and glared at the king. "Don't hurt her," he said before running out the door.

Wolf glanced at the door then to her. "It's good to see my grandfather so full of life again, thank you." Wolff stepped back, and Ridge was there in front of her in seconds.

"Wow, you move fast," Catarina said as Little Tee turned and peeked at the man as he knelt down in front of them.

"So much pain coming from you, little one," Ridge said. "But your new mommy will help you." The man turned his gaze onto her. "You truly are special. In our world, you would be honored for your healing ways."

Catarina frowned. "I don't have any healing ways."

"Oh, but you do, inside your heart. All you have to do is touch the person, and your calmness surrounds them. It's no wonder these three little ones have formed the bond so fast. Are you ready?" he asked, and she nodded, still not believing a word he said. Her heal? Nope.

The man laughed. "Relax, it's not that kind of healing. Think of it like spiritually," he said right before he placed a hand over her chest, right above her heart.

Now, she really was glad she'd told Arad to leave

"Do not think for one minute I don't know he has his hand on you," Arad growled.

She looked up, and sure enough, Gunner and

Arad were there in the doorway. "That was quick," she said.

"Catarina, I want you to think of your girls, call them, reach out to them," Ridge said, and again, she frowned, not understand anything.

But she took a deep breath, closed her eyes, picturing her babies, *Jasmine, Poppy*, she whispered to them in her mind. *"Momma loves you. We're coming, babies, show us where you're at, please."*

Once more, Catarina got that fluttering in her chest. "Got them!" Ridge said, standing up and scaring the living crap out of her.

"We have to go now. I can take ten men with me, my son can take ten, also. Get them here now; there is no time," Ridge said and turned to look at her. "They are weak but alive."

"He hurt them, didn't he?" she asked but already knew the answer when she looked into his eyes.

She must have whimpered, because Romy, Marcus, and even Little Tee moved to her, rubbing their hands on her. Catarina looked up as Arad came over, standing in front of her. "Kill him." was all she said, and Arad nodded.

* * *

Arad wasn't prepared for what he was seeing. The lab full of people half-alive. It had taken them thirty minutes to kill anyone associated with this horrific scene. Not only had Wolf and his men come, but so had Gunner's father and a few of his men, who had shown up just as they were preparing to come.

So far, the one that claimed to be his woman's father had not been found, and by the looks of it, no one was inside the lab now. Either they had slipped away while there had been fighting, or he hadn't been here, which is what he believed. Because Arad had a feeling, he wouldn't have left the twins alive otherwise.

"He's here, my brother," Gunner said, next to him, Gunner's father moving off in another direction as he followed Ridge.

"Go, we'll speak later. Right now, I want to get all of these people out of here and back where it's safe. So we can heal them, at least on the outside," Arad said, moving around a corner and stopping.

His stomach flipped, the smell of death clung in the air. Muffled cries could be heard behind the wooden and steel doors. "How could anyone do this? To children let alone," Arad growled as the first doors opened and Ridge stepped in.

On a dirty bed lay a little girl, skin and bones. She looked over, and her eyes met his.

"I'll hunt him until I die," Arad snarled and moved to the little one. "I'm here to take you to your mommy. Are you Poppy or Jasmine?" he asked, kneeling down.

"Poppy," she mouthed as Ridge leaned down, handing him a bottle of something.

"Have her drink all of this before you move her. It will help heal her faster and contains lots of protein for her. I'll go get her sister. I've also called in help. There is no way we are going to be able to get to all of these people. We'll take them to our world where there will be no threat; they can heal in peace then decide if they want to come back."

Arad reached over and placed his hand on Ridge. "Let it be known, any and all can come live in our small town, also. They will be welcome. We can all heal together," Arad said.

"They will be told." Ridge left and moved across the hall as Arad placed his arm under the little one's head, holding the straw up to her mouth.

"Drink, Poppy, let me tell you who I am." For five minutes, he sat allowing Poppy to drink the concoction Ridge had given her. When he had told her that they would be living with him and three other children, she had smiled.

When the drink was done, he carefully scooped her up in his arms.

"You're going to be our daddy?" she asked, laying her head on his chest as Ridge brought in the other little girl in pretty much the same condition.

"Jasmine heard every word you said. Let's take these two back so I can come back and help the others," Ridge said.

"Gunner?" Arad asked.

"They have found his brother, and it's not good, but he'll live. He is coming back to your house," Ridge said, as once more in seconds they appeared in one of the bedrooms that was right next to their room.

"I thought it best to bring them here," Ridge said, and Arad nodded.

The bedroom door opened, and he heard Catarina's cry. Both girls looked up. Tears rolled down their cheeks as they called for their momma.

Gently, they placed them on the bed. Warm, soft nightgowns covered their little bodies. He looked up at Ridge. "Thank you. I owe you much."

"No, but you are right, this has to stop." With those words, Ridge vanished, leaving Catarina, his three grandchildren, who had come in and were talking to the children now, and him.

After tucking them into the bed, he sat on the floor with Catarina, holding her as she cried silently, refusing to leave her babies. Even Little Tee had tears in her eyes and was now curled up close to Poppy in the bed.

All three children had taken to the twins instantly. Yes, their family would need time and help, but together, they would make it.

The bedroom door creaked open, and Wolf popped his head in. "Gunner's brother is stable and with his family. There were over two hundred children, women, and men there. All have been taken out and the place burned. Rest, all of you, we'll have dinner brought in here for you all."

"Thank you, Wolf," Catarina said. "And please tell Tobie and her family if there is ever anything I can do to help, let me know."

"I will, and Catarina?" Wolf called, and she looked up. "I was wrong. The children belong with you two." Wolf glanced at his grandfather. "I brought back two little boys. From what Ridge informed me, their parents had been killed."

"Tobie?" Arad asked.

Wolf smiled. "She hasn't left their side. Tobie had begged for me to bring them home, and I couldn't refuse her or them."

Arad nodded. "I'm very proud of you, Wolf. Congrats, Daddy," he said, and Wolf snorted, closing the door.

Arad looked around the room and settled back against the wall, watching his children slowly fall asleep. In his arms, his warrior woman, who had given him his life back and he was bound to make sure not one person ever hurt his family again.

Catarina rubbed her cheek on his chest. "You can't promise that, and I don't want you to put that much on yourself. We will all watch and protect each other," she said and looked up at him. "Love you, my wild man,"

He smiled. "Love you too, my warrior woman." He placed a kiss on her forehead. "Rest, it's been a long day."

Chapter One

Isabella Garret didn't move. She was not where she should have been. What happen? What did she do now? Did she once more fall and bang her head being the klutz she was? The last she remembered she had been reading her book when... "Shots!"

She sat up in a bed and stared around a bedroom that was massive and stunning, but so not hers.

"Easy, my Isabella, you don't want to rip open the wound," a voice behind her said.

Slowly, Isabella turned and stared at the hottest man she had ever seen in her life, and she had seen quite a few at the crossing. She shook her head. "Who are you? Where am I? And what wound?" She looked down and squeaked, realizing she was naked.

Snatching up the cover to her chest, Isabella took a deep breath as the man came and sat on the edge of the bed. That is when she noticed that not only was he hot, but he also smelled good and that he was not human.

That is when she felt them, sharp teeth. Her gaze flashed to his. "What did you do?"

He reached over and took one of her hands. "I

had no choice, you would have died yesterday if I hadn't brought you over to my world. I couldn't allow my mate to die."

She pulled her hand away from his, holding it up. "Wait! I'm like you? Drink blood to live? Mate? Okay, I need to wake up now." She reached over and pinched herself, flinching. "Yep, I'm awake." Isabella moaned, flopping back down on the pillow. "Ouch," she said, lifting the blanket, and for the first time seeing the patch of gauze on her chest; his story was ringing true.

"Wait, mate? Is that..." Her hand flew around, pointing to him then to her. "You and I?" she squeaked. "Nope, there is no way that is possible!"

He laughed. "And why isn't it possible? By the way, my name is Gunner Agoston, and you are in my best friend's home. We brought you here to make sure you were safe as you healed and changed. But I did leave word that you were with us and a contact number in case you had family. Do you have family?"

Isabella laughed. "First, it's not possible because, hello, you are... I mean, come on. You could have any woman you wanted. Nope, the Fates wouldn't be that mean to saddle you with the number one klutz on this side of New York. Not to mention that I'm a butterball walking on stilts." She stopped talking when he started to actually growl at her.

He leaned down, his nose touching hers. "I am a very easy-going man. But you will stop this insulting yourself now. You have curves that make my mouth water and my cock hard as a rock. Your black, thick, curly hair is amazing, not to mention the fullness of your breasts and ass. No, honey, you are perfect for me." He frowned at her. "You aren't married, are you?"

"Me? Nope, the last asshole who I dated was a two-timing jerk. Oh, no family, at least, that I know of. I was raised in foster homes mostly. I have to be dreaming," she said.

A soft knock on the bedroom door drew her attention, and a woman popped her head in. "Oh, she's up, good. We're going to have a brunch in the family room if you two would like to join us. I'm Catarina, supposedly Gunner's sister or niece or whatever. Ouch, damn it, Arad, stop that."

"Then quit being noisy and come on, the little ones are starving." The man growled but looked into the room, smiling. "Don't take too long, old man, and don't scare her. I know you get all grumbly in the morning."

"Arad, get out," Gunner said and threw a pillow at the door.

Isabella smiled, hearing the other man laughing as he shut the door.

"Your aim is getting a little better," the other man yelled.

Gunner shook his head. "As you can see, there is a full house. I can promise you this. The women here will help you with anything if you have any problems. I should warn you, my parents are here. So you might have my mother following you around a little, but right now, she and Dad are with my brother." Gunner looked at the door, and she could feel the sadness coming from him.

She reached over and placed her hand on his arm. "Is something wrong?"

"A human scientist had over two hundred, including my brother, locked up doing experiments on them. Women, children, and men," He sighed. "I'm not going to sugarcoat this. Our world is a mess right now, and you will be protected at all costs, but I promise, you'll want for nothing, Isabella."

About the Author

Trinity Blacio has been writing for the past ten years. She is widowed and has two children, living in Elyria, Ohio. Her favorite things to write and read are paranormal, ménage, science fiction, erotica, and fantasy.

Places to find me.
Website: *http://trinityblacio.com*
Twitter: *https://twitter.com/trinityblacio*
Facebook: *https://www.facebook.com/ trinityblacio*
Goodreads: *https://www.goodreads.com/ author/show/2856931.Trinity_Blacio*